ISBN 0-373-11603-4

9 780373 116034

50299

W9-DGL-078

1640044

HARLEQUIN®

$2.99 11603
November

HARLEQUIN PRESENTS®

KAY THORPE

Past All Reason

"Stop it!"

Her voice was low and ragged. "It's all in the past. I'm not even the same person."

"Yes, you are. No one changes character completely. You've simply learned to act another part, that's all." He put out a hand and slid it behind her neck, drawing her to him to kiss her lingeringly on the mouth. "It's still there," he said softly when he lifted his head again. "All of it."

Tricia couldn't deny it. Just one small word would set the whole affair in motion again. But to what end?

KAY THORPE, an English author, has always been able to spin a good yarn. In fact, her teachers said she was the best storyteller in the school—particularly with excuses for being late! Kay then explored a few unsatisfactory career paths before giving rein to her imagination and hitting the jackpot with her first romance novel. After a roundabout route, she'd found her niche at last. The author is married with one son.

Books by Kay Thorpe

HARLEQUIN PRESENTS
1397—INTIMATE DECEPTION
1446—NIGHT OF ERROR
1501—TROUBLE ON TOUR
1534—LASTING LEGACY
1556—WILD STREAK
1571—LEFT IN TRUST

HARLEQUIN ROMANCE
2151—TIMBER BOSS
2232—THE WILDERNESS TRAIL
2234—FULL CIRCLE

Don't miss any of our special offers. Write to us at the following address for information on our newest releases.

Harlequin Reader Service
P.O. Box 1397, Buffalo, NY 14240
Canadian address: P.O. Box 603,
Fort Erie, Ont. L2A 5X3

KAY THORPE

Past All Reason

Harlequin Books

TORONTO • NEW YORK • LONDON
AMSTERDAM • PARIS • SYDNEY • HAMBURG
STOCKHOLM • ATHENS • TOKYO • MILAN
MADRID • WARSAW • BUDAPEST • AUCKLAND

If you purchased this book without a cover you should be aware that this book is stolen property. It was reported as "unsold and destroyed" to the publisher, and neither the author nor the publisher has received any payment for this "stripped book."

ISBN 0-373-11603-9

PAST ALL REASON

Copyright © 1992 by Kay Thorpe.

All rights reserved. Except for use in any review, the reproduction or utilization of this work in whole or in part in any form by any electronic, mechanical or other means, now known or hereafter invented, including xerography, photocopying and recording, or in any information storage or retrieval system, is forbidden without the written permission of the publisher, Harlequin Enterprises Limited, 225 Duncan Mill Road, Don Mills, Ontario, Canada M3B 3K9.

All characters in this book have no existence outside the imagination of the author and have no relation whatsoever to anyone bearing the same name or names. They are not even distantly inspired by any individual known or unknown to the author, and all incidents are pure invention.

This edition published by arrangement with Harlequin Enterprises B. V.

® and TM are trademarks of the publisher. Trademarks indicated with ® are registered in the United States Patent and Trademark Office, the Canadian Trade Marks Office and in other countries.

Printed in U.S.A.

CHAPTER ONE

'MR SMITH has someone with him at the moment,' announced the receptionist. 'If you'd like to take a seat, Miss...' She paused to glance down at the appointments book open on the desk in front of her. 'Barton.'

Tricia moved to do so, wryly aware that the name of Smith could still elicit a faint pang. Not one she came across all that often, despite the number listed in the telephone directory.

'You're from Profiles, aren't you?' asked the young woman at the desk. 'Going to be filling in for Mr Smith's regular secretary?'

'Hopefully,' Tricia agreed. 'I understand she was taken ill very suddenly?'

The other nodded. 'Emergency appendix operation, so she's out for the next three or four weeks at least. With this European tour coming up, I suppose the bureau was the only resort.'

'Couldn't one of the other secretaries be spared?' asked Tricia. 'There must be quite a number in a company the size of this.'

'None Mr Smith apparently thought suitable. His has to be capable of taking on a whole lot more than just the nine-till-five work—especially when he's travelling. Barbara always says it's like being a wife without any of the advantages.'

Tricia raised a quizzical eyebrow. 'Is that a fact?'

The girl laughed. 'I doubt if the MD would complicate his life by taking a personal advantage, if that's what you're thinking. I imagine he has enough women at his beck and call. All he requires is total dedication to the job.'

Tricia said mildly, 'With one's own social life of secondary importance. He won't be the first I've worked for who was that way inclined.'

'Have you been with the bureau long?'

'Almost a year.'

'Good rates of salary?'

'Very. Profiles needs to offer the right kind of incentive to attract the right kind of people.'

'Of which you're one, of course.'

Tricia gave no sign of having noted the faint gibe. 'I have the qualifications, yes.' She glanced at the leather-strapped watch on her wrist, checking the time it gave against the wall clock. 'I'm either five minutes fast, or that's slow. What do you make it?'

'You're right and that's wrong,' came the answer without over-much concern. 'I'll get the electrician up to alter it.' She caught the change of expression in the green eyes opposite, and shook her head. 'Not my job.'

Which said it all, thought Tricia drily. Definitely not Profiles material!

Applying to be taken on their lists herself eleven months ago, she had been impressed by their attention to detail. The clients who applied to Profiles for temporary staff wanted the best and were willing to pay for it, so the best had to be supplied.

The reason she had given for leaving her permanent post had elicited a ready sympathy from the middle-aged but by no means over-the-hill woman who ran the central London branch. Sexual harassment was an occupational hazard of secretarial work, unfortunately, she had declared. The very fact that a secretary was more often than not hired as much on the strength of her looks as her ability underlined the issue. Any such approach by one of their clients, Tricia had been assured, would be dealt with severely.

That aside, this job promised to be quite a challenge. If she met with approval she would need to start right away if she was to have any hope of being *au fait* with all requirements by this time next week.

Most of the actual travelling arrangements would already have been made, of course. It should simply be a case of substituting her name for that of the usual incumbent. They would, she understood, be out of the country for two weeks, visiting Amsterdam, Berlin, Zurich, Milan and Paris. As managing director, Mr Smith would in all probability make such trips on a fairly regular basis.

The intercom buzzer sounded, and the receptionist nodded across at her. 'You can go up now. Top floor. The lift is right over there.'

Hardly to be missed considering it was in plain view, Tricia reflected. The main doors opened as she got to her feet, to admit a couple of young executive types who were greeted by the receptionist with familiarity. They were also taking the lift. Stepping into the cage ahead of them, Tricia gave the pair a cool smile as she turned, aware of their frank appraisal.

Her particular combination of dark brown hair, green eyes and fine-boned features had an effect even the rather severe styling of the first failed to fully dispel, as she knew to her cost. How they might have reacted to the flowing blonde tresses she had once sported, she hated to think. Men were apt to take any female purely at face value—as she also knew to her cost.

Chosen with deliberation, the dark grey suit she was wearing at least concealed the curves which had driven her last boss to apparent distraction. There were times when being a sweater-girl—as more than one man had called her—was a distinct disadvantage. Not that stock size twelve was exactly overweight for her height of five feet six. Quality, not quantity, was how someone had once described her body. His name had been Smith too.

She put that latter memory firmly aside. After three years he was of no importance to her. Considering the time element, it seemed unlikely that she would be turned down for this job. Profiles had no one else immediately available who might be better qualified.

The two young men got off at the fifth floor. Continuing to the seventh, Tricia found herself stepping out on to thick green carpet which stretched like a perfectly laid and mown lawn on either hand. With no one around from whom to ask directions, she opted for the right, moving with a confidence born of long practice along the wide corridor past several mahogany doors until she reached the one inscribed with the name she sought.

Hand on the knob, she stood for a long moment gazing at the initials L.J. with a sudden tautness in her chest. Just another coincidence, of course, she assured herself. Lots of male names began with the letter L. Leigh Smith was in the past. Gone, if not quite as forgotten as she liked to believe. She was a totally different person now from that recklessly inclined twenty-two-year-old who had splashed out a major proportion of her inheritance on a cruise to the West Indies. Three and a half thousand pounds just to play at being rich for the space of three weeks—to say nothing of what she had spent on clothes. Not that she would have regretted a penny of it if Leigh hadn't come into her life.

The outer office was the one she would be using herself if taken on. At present the chair behind the computer work station was occupied by a young woman around her own age whose piquant features were creased in lines of stress as she studied the VDU in front of her.

'I've pressed the delete key by mistake,' she announced in tones of despair. 'A whole two hours' work gone!'

Tricia moved round behind her to look at the screen where the directory was displayed. 'Don't you have back-up?'

'I didn't get round to it,' confessed the girl. 'I'm only standing in for Barbara until the temp arrives. I never used WordPerfect before. Mr Smith is going to go spare if I have to start all over again. I'm supposed to have a print-out ready about ten minutes from now.'

'I might be able to help,' offered Tricia. 'I've used this system.'

'Feel free,' came the ready invitation. 'You can't do any more harm than I've already done.'

Tricia took the seat she vacated. 'What was the file called?'

'Phase Seven GT,' the other supplied. She watched hopefully as Tricia ran swift light fingers over the keys, gasping with relief when a final press of the retrieve key brought the deleted file up on screen again. 'Oh, wonderful! What did you do?'

'Renamed the automatic save file to allow access. You might have lost half a page or so, depending on the time set, but it's better than having to re-enter the whole lot.'

'You're telling me! I didn't even know there was an automatic save. You're a life-saver!' She held out a hand. 'I'm Pauline Howe.'

'Tricia Barton.'

'Oh, the temp!' Pauline looked even more relieved. 'Thank heaven for that! Now I can get back to my own job.'

She gave a start as the intercom buzzed, and leaned over quickly to depress the lighted switch. 'Yes, Mr——'

'Go and see where this Miss Barton got to, will you?' ordered a brusque male voice. 'It's been almost ten minutes since I sent down.'

'She just arrived,' said Pauline hastily. 'I'll send her right in.'

Straightening, she pulled a wry face in Tricia's direction. 'Sorry about that.'

Tricia kept her expression under tight control, fighting the urge to turn tail and run. Different in tone though it had been from the last time she had heard it, the depth and timbre of the voice was the same. In another moment or two she would be face to face with the man who had taken her heart three years ago and smashed it into pieces. Leigh Smith, no other. How on earth did she handle this situation?

By confronting it head-on, that was how, came the swiftly decisive response. He hadn't known how she felt about him. So far as he was concerned she had just been a shipboard affair. If he himself found the situation untenable then that would be that. Mrs Carrington would simply have to find him someone else.

Pauline showed her through to the inner office, announcing her name in the prescribed manner. Sumptuous was Tricia's initial impression of the large and beautifully furnished room. A floor-to-ceiling, wall-to-wall window afforded a magnificent view out over the city.

The man seated behind the ultra-modern desk had hair a shade or two darker than her own. Thick, and crisply styled, it glinted with health and vitality in the bright June sunlight. Tricia could recall every detail of those firmly moulded features in close-up: the clean-cut line of his jaw, the wide, sensual mouth, the taut stretch of smooth brown skin over hard cheekbones and eyes which could change from their customary steely grey to the heart-jerking flame of desire. He would be around thirty-five now, she calculated. Married, no doubt—although she could see no framed photographs on the desk.

'It took you long enough to find your way up here,' he observed.

Tricia took a hold on herself, moving forward across what felt like an acre of cream carpet to sit down in the chair he indicated. 'To find the right office, perhaps,' she agreed with surprising calm. 'But I was here in the building before the appointed time.'

Dark brows lifted as he registered the touch of irony. He studied her with new interest, eyes narrowing a little. 'That's good to hear,' he returned equably. 'I need someone I can rely on to be there when required.'

Tricia allowed pent-up breath to escape slowly. He didn't remember her. Not as yet, anyway. Allowing for both the change in her appearance and the time that had elapsed, she supposed there was no real reason why he should connect her with the girl he had known on board the *Capucine*. She had called herself Emma for the duration of that voyage because it had seemed more up-market a name at the time. She had been a very young and naïve twenty-two in many ways. At the very least, Leigh had cured her of that.

'I'm prepared to be available whenever needed,' she responded. 'Always providing, of course, that I pass muster.'

Leigh inclined his head. 'Taking both the time element and your excellent qualifications into consideration, I'd say that was a foregone conclusion. You come highly recommended by Profiles. They never let us down yet.' He added briskly, 'I'm assuming you can start right away?'

'I came prepared for it,' she said.

'Good. Pauline can show you where everything is before she goes back downstairs. You'll find the itinerary for the trip on your desk. It was only decided on a couple of days ago, so Barbara didn't have a chance to organise travel arrangements. If you contact each branch office they'll see to the hotel reservations themselves.' He glanced down at the sheet of paper in front of him. 'You speak both French and Italian, I see. Fluently?'

'Well enough to get by,' she returned. 'Mrs Carrington tells me you speak four languages yourself.'

'Adequately,' he agreed on a dry note. 'Between the two of us we should be able to cope with any eventuality that might arise.'

Tricia took that statement as dismissal. She got to her feet, willing herself to stay cool, calm and collected as the grey eyes appraised her.

'Is the Tricia short for Patricia?' he asked unexpectedly.

'No, just Tricia,' she said. 'My parents preferred it.'

'You still live with them?'

She shook her head. 'They're both dead. I have a flat out at Kingston at present.'

Leigh made no attempt to offer meaningless condolences. He said instead, 'I'd prefer you to be on closer call this next week. Book yourself into the Savoy. To be charged to the company, naturally.'

Not about to dispute the order, Tricia nodded. 'I'll need to fetch some things, of course.'

'Of course. Take one of the pool cars after lunch and go before rush-hour. You do drive?'

'Yes.' She could have added that she had never driven in central London before, but didn't. She would brave far worse rather than acknowledge trepidation at the thought. A few nights at the Savoy would compensate for any stress the journey might generate. A first there too. 'I'll get started, then,' she said.

She could feel his eyes on her back as she crossed the room to the door. It took a whole lot of control to keep her hand steady as she reached for the knob. Outside again, with the door closed between them, she leaned against the smooth wood for a moment to recover from the strain of the last few minutes.

Pauline was still in residence finishing off the printout. She looked up with an understanding expression.

'Not exactly the relaxing type, is he? Are you staying?'

Tricia summoned a smile and pressed herself away from the door. 'Yes. I'm to start right away.'

'Thank heaven for that! When I saw your face just now, I had my doubts.' She shook her head. 'I don't know how Barbara puts up with the job. He's a total slave-driver!' She gave a sudden sigh. 'Dishy with it, though. He could have his pick of the female staff—including the married ones!'

'But I gather he doesn't?' commented Tricia lightly. 'Mix business with pleasure, I mean.'

'Not that I know of. Barbara doesn't tell tales out of school, but she's hardly his type anyway.'

Tricia made a pretence of studying the layout of the office. 'What would you call his type?'

'Blonde, beautiful and twenty-something, judging from those he's been seen with.'

'No Mrs Smith?'

'Not so far.' Pauline gave her a bland look. 'Fancying your chances?'

Tricia laughed. 'I'm not marriage-inclined.'

'Who's talking about marriage?'

'I'm not interested in any other form of attachment either. At least, not with a man I work for.'

'Taken due note of,' came the disembodied voice from the intercom. 'If the two of you have finished your discussion, perhaps you'd like to bring me in the file you were working on, Pauline.'

The click of the released switch came through loud and clear. Pauline gazed at Tricia in dismay. 'I left the line open,' she declared unnecessarily, switching off now when it was too late. 'Oh, lord, what do I say?'

Tricia came to a swift if not particularly ready decision. 'Give me the file. I'll take it through.'

The other girl handed it over with alacrity. 'I'm not arguing.'

Leaving her handbag and gloves on the desk, Tricia took a deep breath before going over to tap lightly on the door via which she had so recently exited from the inner sanctum. Leigh was sitting where she had left him, busy writing something on what appeared to be the same document containing her details.

'If that's my dismissal I can hardly blame you,' she said levelly. 'I was thoroughly out of order.'

He sat back to look at her, expression difficult to define. 'A disinclination towards office affairs is hardly grounds for dismissal,' he returned. 'My only objection is to the place and time you chose to make the statement. If you've any doubts regarding my possible conduct while we're in Europe, I'd prefer to hear them first hand.'

So that was the only bit he had heard, she thought in relief. 'It was a joke,' she claimed. 'Not meant to be taken seriously. I'm sorry, anyway. It shouldn't have happened.'

'No, it shouldn't.' There was a pause while he studied her, that same faint line appearing between his brows. 'We never met before, did we?'

Her heart missed a beat, then steadied again. Somehow she kept her face from reflecting her inner perturbation. 'I don't imagine so. It's doubtful if we move in the same circles.'

'Just a thought. You seem somehow familiar.' He paused again. 'Which circles *do* you move in?'

'Local. I rarely come into town for entertainment.'

'You were with Grant-Dawson a year ago, I see. What made you decide to go into bureau work?'

'I needed a change,' she said shortly. 'Do you have my whole CV there?'

One dark brow flicked upwards at her tone. 'I requested it. You're going to be privy to a lot of confidential information over the next few weeks. I needed someone with the right kind of working background. You've come a long way since business training college—especially in the last three years. It seemed odd that you'd choose to take temporary work rather than permanent, that's all.'

'Profiles offer the right kind of financial incentive along with a change of scene every few weeks or months,' Tricia acknowledged. 'It's all good experience.'

'To what eventual end?'

She lifted her shoulders. 'Remains to be seen.'

'But with marriage a definite no-go area?'

Green eyes met grey, holding the satirical gaze with an effort. 'Not all women are out to land a man, Mr Smith. I'm perfectly self-sufficient.'

'At the present time perhaps. What happens when you reach your thirties? Do you think you'll still be content with the single life?'

'*You* obviously are,' she pointed out coolly, and elicited a derisive smile.

'Rather different for a man. One of the facts of life you feminists can't get round.'

'I'm no feminist,' she denied. 'Not the way you mean it, at any rate.'

'But you do believe in equal opportunity regardless of sex?'

'That's another matter altogether.' He was goading her deliberately, she knew, and she was determined not to rise to it. 'There are certain jobs no woman could tackle for the simple reason that she lacks the muscle power, but we're capable of taking on most vocations.'

'Including my job?'

'With the necessary experience, yes. You'd hardly expect another man to step straight into your shoes without it.'

She was giving back gibe for gibe, closing her mind to the memory of a time when action had spoken so much louder than words between them. As a lover, Leigh had left no part of her unsatisfied. His ardour in that final week of the cruise had transported her to realms she had never imagined could exist; his whole attitude had been that of a man as much in love with her as she with him.

The crunch when he calmly took his leave of her without so much as a suggestion that they meet again had been devastating. A holiday romance for him, a long-lasting agony of heartache and regret for her. She should hate him for what he had done to her, but where was the point? The best thing to do was forget it—the way he had forgotten it. Just do the job and then move on. That had been the pattern of her life for the past eleven months, and she liked it that way.

'You wanted this,' she said now, placing the file on the desk. 'I'll go and get on with things.' She glanced at her watch. 'Coffee in ten minutes?'

'Fine.' He sounded businesslike again himself. 'I've a luncheon appointment at twelve-thirty, so give me a reminder on the hour if I'm not out by then.'

Pauline was waiting in mingled anxiety and curiosity for her return. 'You were a long time,' she said. 'What happened?'

Tricia smiled and shrugged. 'Not a lot. He only overheard the last bit, so you're in the clear. I apologised for the untoward comments, and that was that.'

'You've more nerve than I have,' came the wry response. 'I wouldn't have known what to say! Do you think you could be taking a look round on your own while I slip down to the cloakroom? I'm practically on my last legs!'

'Then you'd better go,' Tricia agreed. 'I'll be fine.'

She waited until the other girl had left the room before making any move to reach for the telephone directory. First the Savoy—if they had a room available at short notice. The tourists were back in force after the decline over the past couple of years or so. Central London hotels tended to be booked solid from May onwards.

She was lucky enough to take over a recently received cancellation for the coming week. Satisfaction at both ends, she thought humorously as she replaced the receiver. The promised coffee next, then she would start making the necessary arrangements for the European trip.

Facilities for making coffee and tea and the odd snack were contained in an alcove behind louvred doors. She used the smaller of the two cafetières, and set out a silver tray with fine china cup and saucer and a choice from the box of Scottish shortcake biscuits she found in the cupboard.

Everything here was first class, she acknowledged. Not that she would have expected anything else from a company as big and powerful as the Brinkland Corporation. For Leigh Smith to have made managing director by the age of thirty-five, he had to be brilliant. He hadn't talked about his background three years ago any more than he had asked after hers. They had both had other things on their minds.

She had to stop this reminiscing, Tricia told herself severely at that point. If she wanted to see this job through—and she did—she had to blank out the whole episode. The girl she had been three years ago was buried beneath layers of acquired poise and proficiency. Men were of relatively little importance in her life at present, and she intended to keep it that way until that special someone came along—if ever. Unrequited love was too painful an emotion for her to risk the experience again.

Leigh was studying the file she had taken in earlier when she went through with the coffee. He nodded his thanks as she slid the tray on to the desk where the cup could be reached without stretching too far, yet stood in little danger of being knocked over accidentally. Tricia had seen important documents ruined before by a careless movement.

'How did you know I took neither sugar nor milk?' he asked suddenly as she started to turn away.

She froze for a second, mentally cursing the totally involuntary quirk of memory. 'Pauline told me, of course,' she claimed.

'I shouldn't have thought she'd know my tastes either, considering she's only been up here a couple of hours.'

Tricia forced herself to look him in the eye, to smile lightly. 'Perhaps Barbara left a note. Is it important?'

'Just a passing curiosity,' he acknowledged. 'I hope you're more proficient at word processing than Pauline appears to be. This whole thing will need to be redone.'

Tricia held out a hand. 'I'll see to it as soon as I've finished organising reservations—unless you need it right away, that is?'

He shook his head. 'It will have to be tomorrow morning now. I'm going to be out all afternoon. You'll need the time yourself to get out to Kingston and back. You managed to get in at the Savoy?'

'Just,' she acknowledged. 'Not that I wouldn't have been quite happy somewhere a little less up-market.'

One dark brow lifted sardonically. 'Only a little?'

She refused to be drawn. 'I like comfort as much as the next person. I'm just not accustomed to luxury.'

'You will be by the time we get back from Europe,' Leigh returned. 'Nothing but the best for Brinkland executive personnel. It's in the contract.'

The clamour of the telephone cut through any reply Tricia might have made to that observation. Another line Pauline had left open. She moved automatically to lift the extension receiver, and said crisply, 'Managing director's office?'

'What happened to Barbara?' asked a male voice.

'I'm afraid she's on sick leave. May I know who's calling, please?'

'James Bryant. Is Leigh in?'

'Just one moment.' She covered the earpiece with a hand to look at the man behind the desk. 'James Bryant?'

The grey eyes held a mocking light. 'Impressive efficiency! Yes, I'll speak to him.'

'Putting you through now, sir,' she said, and handed over the instrument, turning immediately to leave.

'How's it going?' she heard Leigh say as she crossed the room, followed almost immediately by a laugh. 'She's all of that! From Profiles, if you're interested in acquiring one of your own.'

Tit for tat, she thought wryly, closing the door on him without glancing round. Except that he had known *she* could hear *him*. And all of what? she couldn't help wondering.

Pauline had returned and was sorting out the welter of paperwork covering the desk. She eyed the file in Tricia's hand in rueful recognition.

'I messed it up, didn't I?'

'Don't worry about it,' Tricia consoled. 'You can hardly be expected to step straight into someone else's shoes.'

'It's what you're doing,' the other pointed out.

'I'm used to it. It was hardly fair to land you with all this in the first place.'

'When I'm so obviously not up to it?' Pauline laughed and shook her head as Tricia began to form a denial. 'I'd be the first to agree. I was only supposed to be standing in to answer the phone et cetera until you arrived, then Mr Smith landed that on me.'

'You didn't try to tell him you'd never used the system before?'

'He didn't give me the chance. To be honest, I'm not going to be all that much use to you when it comes to general routine either. Barbara only ever trusted one other person to take over when she went on holiday, and she retired last month.'

Tricia said curiously, 'She chose her own stand-in?'

'Oh, yes. Fifteen years with the company—eight of them as secretary to the MD—gives her a lot of clout. Mr Smith inherited her when he took over a couple of years ago. His father is chairman, you know. I suppose one day he'll step into those shoes, too.'

Not just a company director, then, Tricia reflected, but probably a major shareholder into the bargain. Not that it made any difference to her. Once Barbara returned, she would be on her way again—and no regrets.

'I'll cope,' she said. 'That's what I'm here for.'

'In that case I'll get back to my own department,' Pauline declared thankfully. 'There's a very good staff restaurant on the second floor if you fancy meeting up later for lunch?'

'Thanks, but I'll probably make myself a sandwich,' Tricia responded. 'There's a tin of salmon in the cupboard, plus a loaf and some salad in the fridge.'

'Yes, Barbara rarely goes out to lunch. She's still a Miss at thirty-seven. I suppose her whole life revolves around her job.' Pauline pulled a face. 'I'd hate to think I was going to end up like that!'

She too, thought Tricia. Neither did she intend to end up like that. There was time enough for everything yet. Twenty-five was far too soon to start feeling panicky about the future.

CHAPTER TWO

WITH so much to be done, the rest of the morning passed all too quickly. By eleven-fifty Tricia had contacted all five European offices and asked for accommodation to be arranged for the dates given.

All the people to whom she spoke were fluent in English. Unlike the last multi-national company she had worked for, where activity pending a visit by one of the upper hierarchy had reached frenetic proportions, no one seemed particularly disturbed by the news.

Seats were booked on a flight leaving Heathrow for Amsterdam at 10.05 the following Monday morning, with provisional reservations made between cities: time-tables didn't always work out exactly to plan. Sitting back in her seat after putting down the telephone receiver at last, Tricia stretched cramped limbs and allowed herself a small glow of satisfaction. So far, so good.

What remained now was to sort out the paperwork on her desk and leave the office in order ready for a clear start tomorrow morning. Getting here from the Savoy was going to be a doddle compared with the usual fraught journey by train. Four nights in one of London's top hotels certainly wasn't to be sneezed at either.

She would return home Friday night, of course, and meet up with Leigh at Heathrow on Monday morning. That would give her the weekend to sort things out with Neil. He was becoming far too possessive, and she had no intention of being possessed—neither physically nor emotionally. If he couldn't accept the limitations of their friendship, then it was best that it ended.

Catching sight of her watch, with the fingers standing together on the midday hour, she reached hastily for the intercom switch. 'It's twelve o'clock, Mr Smith,' she announced when he answered the buzz. 'Your luncheon appointment.'

'I'll be right out,' he said.

He emerged bare moments later, broad of shoulder and lean of hip in the superbly tailored grey suit. Tricia had forgotten how tall he was—how lithe when he moved. He had been recuperating from a virus attack which had left him several pounds underweight when she had known him. He had regained that, she noted, but certainly no more. Everything about him suggested total fitness and vitality.

She swallowed on the sudden hard lump in her throat as her eyes met his. Telling herself he no longer meant anything to her was one thing, convincing herself something else again. It would have been wiser to find some excuse to turn down the job once she had realised who he was.

'I'll see you in the morning,' he said. 'Bright and early. I'm always here nine sharp myself.'

Which meant she had better beat him to it, Tricia gathered. No problem there. She was used to rising at six-thirty.

'Enjoy your lunch,' she said, and saw his mouth widen briefly.

'It's purely business today, so no great expectations.'

The office seemed empty after he had gone. Try as she might, Tricia couldn't stop her thoughts from turning back over the years, recalling the scintillating excitement of standing on deck to watch the gap between ship and quayside slowly widen as the voyage got under way...

'Next stop, the Azores,' said the man leaning on the rails near by. He smiled as Tricia turned her head towards him, eyes frankly appreciative as they rested on her face and free-flowing mane of streaked blonde hair. 'Leigh Smith.'

Her return smile came easily, naturally, the new name equally so. 'Emma Barton.'

'Travelling alone?'

She laughed. 'All alone! And you?'

'The same.' He sounded anything but disconsolate about it. 'Why don't we join forces for a drink to celebrate the start of what promises to be a better voyage than I anticipated?'

Tricia allowed herself a brief hesitation, savouring the knowledge that he obviously found her as attractive as she found him. Early thirties, she judged, and accustomed to the best in life. It was there in his manner, in the cut of his pale grey trousers and light tweed jacket. What he was doing on his own on board the *Capucine*, she couldn't imagine. He was hardly the introvert preferring his own company.

'That sounds a very good idea,' she agreed, casting any doubt aside. If she was going to play the part at all, this was as good a time to start as any.

She was here to sample the way the other half lived, with no intention of allowing anyone to know how unaccustomed she was to having money to burn. The distant relative from whom she had inherited almost twenty thousand pounds as the only surviving member of the family would probably have been horrified by the use to which she was putting so large a percentage of her capital, but she was unlikely ever to have such an opportunity again. The *Capucine* was no package-deal ship. She carried a superior type of clientele. This man belonged the way she wanted to belong—even if it was only for a limited period.

Pacing alongside her as she moved towards the companionway, he made her feel almost petite. Well over six feet in height, she reckoned, and with a breadth of shoulder that suggested muscular power beneath the tweed jacket. She was wearing a jacket herself against the spring chill of the Southampton air; pale green in her case, to tone with the simple green and white striped cotton shirtwaister that had cost her more than any garment she had ever purchased in her life before.

Good clothes felt as good as they looked, she acknowledged now. They imparted a whole new kind of confidence. A month ago this Leigh Smith probably wouldn't have given her a second glance.

They went to the smaller of the two bars on Veranda deck. With the time coming up to five o'clock, Tricia asked for a dry martini, but couldn't bring herself to eat the olive.

'They're not much to my taste either,' Leigh commented when she put it aside. 'I'll remember to order without next time.'

Tricia laughed. 'You're so sure there's going to be a next time?'

'Of course.' He was smiling himself, grey eyes assured. 'You don't think I'm going to let anyone else monopolise the best-looking girl on board!'

'You've barely had chance to make comparisons yet,' she pointed out. 'Isn't it a little early to start making commitments?'

'Not for me,' he declared with flattering certainty. 'You'd stand out in any crowd. I only started taking an interest in this cruise when I saw you coming on board earlier.'

She regarded him with head on one side, thrilling to the mere fact of being here like this with a man like this. 'So why are you on it at all?'

His shrug was light. 'Doctor's orders. I had some kind of flu bug which left me what he likes to call "run-down". The sea air is supposed to set me up again. It seemed a total waste of three weeks—until I spotted you coming up the gangway.' The smile came again, heart-stirring in its sheer impact. 'Did you ever visit the West Indies before?'

Tricia shook her head. 'One of the reasons I decided to take this particular cruise,' she acknowledged truthfully. 'I hate visiting places more than once.' Which was true too, so far as it went. The fact that she had travelled no further afield than France and Italy before this was beside the point.

'Only one of the reasons?' quizzed Leigh.

Her shrug was as light as his had been. 'I needed to get away for a while.'

'Man trouble?'

She hadn't intended using that line, but one was as good as another. Green eyes met grey without a flicker. 'Not any more.'

'Good,' he said. 'So we're both of us heartwhole and fancy-free.'

A statement Tricia was able to agree with right then, but that was only the beginning.

The first week of the cruise went by on swift wings. Leigh monopolised almost every waking moment of her time. They formed the habit of meeting at seven every morning for a jog around the deck, followed by a cup of bouillon beside one of the pools before parting to shower and change for breakfast.

Leigh had a stateroom on the upper deck. Comfortable and roomy as she had found her own cabin on the deck below, Tricia was knocked sideways by the sheer luxury of the other. The sleeping area was contained behind folding doors, the living quarters alone larger than her whole bed-sitting room back home.

'Not bad, I suppose,' Leigh acknowledged when she commented admiringly the first time he invited her back for a drink after dinner. He sounded as if he hadn't given it all that much thought before that moment. 'You'd have done better booking this deck yourself.'

At considerably more cost, Tricia reflected wryly, murmuring agreement. Money obviously meant little to Leigh. He'd been born into this kind of lifestyle—or so one was bound to assume. She had no intention of allowing him to know that she hadn't. He would probably lose interest altogether if he once realised how far apart their backgrounds really were.

Fortunately, if somewhat oddly, he showed no particular interest in her past, but seemed content simply to enjoy her company here and now. Conversation between them ranged over a wide variety of subjects, in most of which she was well able to hold her own. Intelligence, at least, wasn't a prerogative of the rich.

The first time he kissed her was a revelation. Until the moment, Tricia hadn't known just how wonderful kissing could be. Leigh was an experienced man, not a gauche youth—that was the difference, she supposed. No open-mouth slobbering such as her last and very temporary boyfriend had practised in the fond belief that he was 'turning her on', as he put it, but a tantalising, seductive, slowly increasing assertion until her lips petalled open of their own eager accord to the spine-tingling touch of his tongue.

She was 'turned on' by Leigh without any doubt. From kissing her mouth it was but a short progression to kissing her bared breasts, driving her wild with the sheer eroticism of his caresses. Whatever prudishness she might have possessed went right out of the porthole. With Leigh she felt no sense of reluctance, no inhibition. She revelled in his lovemaking, yearned for it when they were apart or in company. He made her feel the way she had never felt before in her life; the way she was sure she would never feel again about anyone. Falling in love with him was inevitable.

Not that he took immediate advantage of what must have been her obvious readiness to fall in with whatever he wanted of her. They were halfway through the second week of the cruise before he made any serious move towards furthering the relationship.

The ship had docked at Bridgetown, Barbados for a twelve-hour stay. Disdaining to join the organised coach tour of the island, Leigh elected to hire a car and drive the two of them round himself. Tricia wasn't loath to agree. Being alone with Leigh was all she wanted. All she needed.

They ate lunch at a small but exclusive and very expensive beachside restaurant on the west coast, then found themselves a secluded little cove for sunbathing, with swimming to come later after their meal had settled.

'Not a bad way of life, beachcombing in a place like this,' commented Leigh lazily, eyes closed against the sunlight filtering through the palm fronds above. 'I might even consider retiring here when the time comes.'

'That's looking a bit far ahead, isn't it?' laughed Tricia. 'Unless you plan on taking an extra early retirement, that is.'

'That,' he said, 'would depend on the inducements.' He rolled to face her, reaching out a hand to smooth the bare skin of her midriff below the bikini-top, a slow smile curving his lips as he watched her expression change. 'Given a suitable companion, it could be roses all the way!'

Her heartbeats drummed in her ears, muscle and sinew tensing as the long lean fingers traced an intricate, slowly expanding pattern over her fluttering skin. The bikini-bottom was briefer than any she had ever worn in her life before, a mere triangle at the front, shrinking to a thong at the back. She had the figure for it, the woman assistant in the ship's boutique had declared admiringly, and she had somehow found the nerve. Seeing the look in Leigh's eyes when she had stripped off her shorts and T-shirt a few moments ago had made it all worthwhile. Clad only in swimming trunks himself, there had been no way of disguising his arousal—nor had he even attempted to do so by turning away from her.

Not for him, though, the hasty execution. Aroused he might be, uncontrolled he wouldn't allow himself to be. The pause had been deliberate; she realised now—a smouldering interlude calculated to bring them both to fever-pitch before commencing on the act itself. Several times before this his caresses had brought her to a point where she would quite willingly have given herself to him wholly and completely, but he had always been the one to draw back. This time she knew that the moment had come when he wasn't going to draw back.

The sun was blocked out completely as he brought his head down to find her mouth with his in a kiss that stirred

her innermost being. Arms about his neck, she gave
herself up totally to the emotions coursing through her.
The bikini was no barrier to the searching fingers, her
limbs pliable to his touch. She gasped against his lips at
that first intimate intrusion, but there was no thought
in her mind of protestation. She wanted him to know
her in every way there was; to possess her utterly. Wonderful, exciting, darling Leigh!

A stifled cry was drawn from her as she climaxed. Still
kissing her, Leigh brought his hand up the length of her
body to reach behind her and unfasten the thin strings
of her bra. She tremored as he removed the scrap of
material from her, glad of the full firmness of her breasts,
open now to eyes and hands and mouth, all of which
Leigh employed with pleasure for them both.

'Beautiful,' he murmured. 'Every solitary inch of you!'

Tricia made no demur when he slid his hand back
down over her hip to take the narrow band and ease it
away from her. Naked, she felt neither shame nor reticence, only pure delight that the sight of her could elicit
such passion in the grey eyes. She watched with fast-
beating heart as he slid his trunks down his legs and
tossed them aside, knowing a sudden and almost
primitive fear stir in her when he came over her in the
dominant attitude of the male animal.

As if recognising the emotion, he made no immediate
move to enter her, but kissed her back to a point where
her whole body was aflame with longing, with need,
where her limbs opened of their own accord in eager
invitation, hips lifting to facilitate his penetration. There
was none of the half-anticipated pain, just a wonderful
sense of joining, of sliding together to become one whole
person, of total submission to this man she loved with
such overweening passion.

And that was just the beginning. In the moments following she found herself reaching heights she hadn't even imagined could exist. Leigh was in command the whole way through, intent, it seemed, on giving her the utmost pleasure before finally allowing himself the luxury of fulfilment. They climaxed almost together, and lay supine for whole minutes recovering from that final giddy whirl.

As if the world itself was spinning on its axis, thought Tricia dazedly, gazing into the flickering sunlight.

Leigh was the first to make a move, lifting his head to look down at her with a smile on his lips. 'Exquisite,' he said softly. 'Well worth waiting for.'

'Why did you?' she asked without meaning to, and bit her lip as she realised what she was implying.

The smile changed character, a subtle change she couldn't really define. 'Anticipation enhances any event,' he said. 'I prefer the gradual ascent to a swift assault. If we'd got this far last week, we might even be bored with each other by now.'

Never! she thought, but she could only speak for herself, of course. The intimation that he might well have found it so was painful in the extreme.

'It wouldn't have,' she denied. 'Got that far, I mean.'

'It could have.' The statement was made with quiet certainty. 'You were good and ready for it.' He regarded her quizzically as her eyes darkened. 'Why look so unhappy? You're a beautiful, highly sexed young woman. Nothing wrong with that.'

'I don't . . . make a habit of this kind of thing,' Tricia protested.

'I don't imagine you do,' he said. 'Highly sexed doesn't necessarily mean promiscuous. Too many risks this day and age, anyway.' He levered himself away from her,

grimacing a little as he did so. 'Damned sand gets everywhere! We'd better take that swim and get rid of it.'

Tricia sat up as he rose to his feet, wrapping her arms
about her knees in a gesture ridiculously protective considering the circumstances. Apart from the paler strip
about his lower hipline, Leigh was golden bronze all over.
Muscle rippled beneath taut stretched skin as he moved.

He looked down at himself with a wry little smile.
'Recovery rate definitely not up to par,' he commented
lightly. 'But time for everything yet. Are you coming
in?'

Tricia reached automatically for the discarded bikini,
desisting abruptly when he lifted an amused eyebrow.
She found a smile of her own and came slowly to her
feet, conscious of his eyes drifting the length of her body
with an expression in them that she could only describe
as proprietorial. There was no single inch of her that he
didn't know intimately, no secrets left to her except for
those in her heart and mind. Before this cruise was over,
she hoped to share them with him too—and to have them
reciprocated. They were made for each other, the two
of them. Perfectly matched!

The sea was warmer than any she had ever bathed in
before. Laughing, she swam away from Leigh, cutting
through the smooth, crystal-clear water in an exuberance
of mood that lent her arms extra strength. Fast though
she was, he caught up with her inside a hundred or so
feet and seized her by the waist to draw her round to
face him, holding her close against the whole hard length
of his body while he kissed her with a passion surpassing
even that which had gone before.

He was still able to stand on the bottom at this depth,
she realised, although her own feet were clear of the sand
His recovery rate had accelerated on immersion, it

seemed, for he was fully aroused again. Buoyant in the water, Tricia found her limbs adjusting of their own accord to fit themselves to him, felt the exquisite sensation as they joined and became one again. There could never be anything to surpass this, came the fleeting thought before mind and matter merged and the world spun once more under the hot beat of the sun.

It was late when they finally got back to the ship. They sailed at seven for La Guaria on the Venezuelan coast. Dressing for dinner, Tricia luxuriated in memories of the day just gone. She and Leigh were lovers now in every sense of the word. Not just a temporary affair on his part either, she was sure. He had taken his time in making full love to her because he had wanted to get to know her properly first; she could understand and appreciate that desire.

Except that he didn't know her properly, did he? came the thought, bringing a sudden and devastating drop in spirits. She was here under false pretences; even her name was a sham! If they were to continue their relationship once they were back home in England she would have to tell him the truth, of course. There was no way she could keep up the pretence on home ground.

It wouldn't make any difference to him, she told herself firmly at that point. Not the way things were between them. He'd probably consider the whole thing mere foolishness on her part. Which it had been. She could see that now. Changing her name hadn't changed her personality. It was Tricia Barton who had attracted him, Tricia Barton who would continue to attract him. Emma didn't exist.

All the same, she found it difficult to confess to the deception. Every day she seemed to come up with a new reason why she should wait a little longer to tell him the truth. The nights they spent together, usually in Leigh's stateroom. Showering with him was a particular delight. Tricia lost count of the number of times they made love that last week. It seemed that Leigh could no more have enough of her than she of him.

Only when they were within hours of docking at Southampton did she finally begin to discard the rose-coloured spectacles and realise that for Leigh the whole three weeks had been no more than an enjoyable interlude: an attitude that he also seemed to take for granted she shared. Somehow she found the ability to hide her feelings and say goodbye on the quayside with the same insouciance he himself employed. The fact that she no longer needed to confess to the deception was her only comfort, such as it was. There and then she vowed never again to make the same mistake in giving herself to a man on the strength of a one-sided emotion. From here on in she would concentrate on building a career.

Which she had, she reflected, coming back with a jerk to the present day, and with considerable success. She was good at her job, she knew. Three years of dedicated application had seen to that. If her social life had suffered, that was simply the price that had to be paid. One thing she had made sure of: no man had ever been allowed to get close again the way Leigh had.

Meanwhile, time was marching on and she still had to get out to Kingston and back. She would eat lunch at home, she decided. She could be there inside the hour. All she had to do was collect a car from the pool.

It was some relief, on arriving at the basement garage area, to find that Leigh had taken the trouble to phone down and arrange a vehicle for her. She was allocated a three-month-old Vauxhall Cavalier, and left by the security attendant to find her own way out of the place. With an automatic gear-box, she was at least spared the constant changing up and down that the central-city traffic would necessitate. All she had to do now was head for the river at Blackfriars Bridge, then the A3 down to Kingston Hill.

By the time she reached the river she was about ready to jump in. The lunchtime traffic was horrendous for people unaccustomed to threading their own way through. Tricia blessed the automatic gear-box. Without it, she was sure she would have stalled the engine more than once.

It was still busy on the A3, but at least the stream was free-flowing. Her flat was situated on the far side of the river, towards Hampton Wick. She had put down the balance of her inheritance as deposit two years ago, and taken the rest on mortgage. There were times when she found her budget stretched to the limit, though so far she had managed to keep her head above water. Working for Profiles was risky in the sense that there might come a period when no job was available, but so far that hadn't happened. The problem was, Mrs Carrington had assured her when asked the question, finding enough of the right calibre people to fulfil demand.

Decorated throughout in pastel shades, the flat was light and airy and looked larger than it was. Tricia went straight through to the single bedroom and took down her suitcase from an upper cupboard, laying it open on the bed ready to receive the things she was going to need for a four-night stay in the city. She might, she thought, take the opportunity to see a couple of shows while she was on the spot, so she was going to need clothes other than those she wore to work. She was a firm believer, anyway, in covering all eventualities.

Lunch consisted of a tuna salad she had prepared for her evening meal. Nothing she had left in the refrigerator was likely to go off in four days. Milk she bought from the supermarket as needed, so no note was required cancelling deliveries.

She put a message on the answering machine saying she would be back home Friday evening, and also rang Neil's flat to leave a slightly more personal message for him. He wasn't going to be too delighted to have their regular Tuesday-night date cancelled at such short notice, but there was nothing she could do about that. Come the weekend, it was all going to be sorted out with him in any case.

By three o'clock she was on her way back to the city. Taking the car to the Savoy was hardly going to be practical. She would, Tricia decided, return it to the garage and take a taxi down from there. If the weather stayed fine she could even walk to work. That would be a bonus in itself. And next week another bonus in the shape of the European tour. Not exactly a pleasure trip, of course, but there would surely be some free time in which to see the sights.

The main drawback was going to be Leigh himself, she acknowledged ruefully at that point. Circumstances alone would make sure that they spent a great deal of time together. Taking the job on at all had been foolish, but she was stuck with it now and had to make the best of things. Ignoring, or trying to ignore, the attraction he still held for her was going to be the hardest part. Not that he was likely to be making it harder still by treating her as anything other than an employee.

She was rid of the car by four o'clock, and checking in at the Savoy before the half-hour had struck. Shown to her spacious, tastefully decorated and furnished room by a young assistant manager, Tricia felt like royalty. She could live this kind of life quite happily, she thought whimsically.

Tiled in marble—floor and walls—the bathroom was pure Victorian era, the bath itself big enough for two. There was even a telephone on the wall, plus hanging call-cords bearing the tags 'Valet' and 'Maid'. Setting out her toilet things, Tricia was glad that they were of an up-market brand name. They might cost the earth but at least they fitted the venue.

With her clothes unpacked and hung away in one of the two wardrobes, she found herself wondering what to do next. It was still only a little gone half-past five: too early for dinner, a bit too late for afternoon tea. The whole evening stretched before her. Being on one's own in any big city wasn't that much of a sinecure when it came right down to it—especially for a woman. Not just a case of where to go, but of how to get there and back without running into trouble.

The ringing of the telephone startled her because it was the last thing she was expecting. She hadn't told Neil where she would be staying, so it could hardly be him. She moved across to the bed to pick up the receiver from the set on the side-table, and said crisply, 'Yes?'

'You're not in the office now,' mocked the all-too-familiar voice on the other end of the line. 'Try sounding a little less businesslike.' He gave her no time to reply. 'Just checking to make sure you made it OK. No problems?'

Tricia drew in a steadying breath before replying, aware of her increased pulse-rate. 'None at all, thank you.' She added, 'It's good of you to take the trouble, Mr Smith.'

'Barbara calls me Leigh,' he said. 'You'd better do the same. I'm not into protocol.'

'It hardly gives the ideal impression on a professional level, though, does it?' she returned coolly. 'Familiarity breeds contempt, and all that.'

The laugh held genuine amusement. 'I'll take the risk. Where were you thinking of eating dinner?'

The question took her by surprise. She floundered for a moment, robbed of her customary balance. 'I—I'm not sure.'

'Then how about joining forces? I'm staying in town tonight myself. I could do with a little company.'

Tricia had stiffened. She said crisply, 'I'm sure there's no shortage of willing companions in your life!'

'None I feel in the mood for entertaining tonight,' came the reply. 'Call it a simple gesture of thanks for being there when needed.'

'It's my job,' she returned. 'I'm getting well paid for it. No further thanks necessary.'

'Your choice, of course.' He sounded just a little clipped himself now. 'I might mention in passing that we'll be eating together quite a lot over the next two weeks, both alone and with others. I hope you don't make a habit of reading ulterior motives into every move. It could become irksome.' The pause was fleeting, the atmosphere definitely cooler. 'I'll see you in the morning. Don't be late.'

The other receiver went down with an audible thud. Biting her lip, Tricia replaced her own instrument. A simple gesture, he had called it, which might well be true. Except that for her no gesture he made on a personal level could ever be simple.

She couldn't go on with this, she decided numbly. She'd been an idiot to even contemplate doing so. She would go in to the office in the morning, yes, but it would be to tell him that he would have to find someone else to accompany him to Europe.

CHAPTER THREE

MORNING saw no change of decision. Awake at six-thirty, Tricia was showered and dressed by the time Room Service delivered the breakfast ordered the previous evening.

On a morning as fine as this one she could walk to the office quite comfortably from here. A pleasant change from the pushing and shoving that went into gaining a seat, or even standing-room, on the train. That she would be back to doing just that after today was something of a damper, but no way could she contemplate spending the next four weeks in Leigh's company. Not now. Too many shades of the man she had known so intimately.

The sun felt hot already on her skin as she moved along the Strand in the general flow. Whether it was convenient or not, she wouldn't, Tricia decided, choose to live in central London full time. A job overseas for a spell might be an idea worth considering—always providing it was somewhere politically stable, which cut down the options somewhat.

She reached her destination at eight-thirty to find the receptionist she had met the previous day chatting with the security guard. Youngish and muscle-bound, the latter gave Tricia an interested once-over as she passed, then made a *sotto voce* remark which drew a smothered laugh from his companion. Typical of the species, reflected Tricia drily in the lift. His kind saw women one way and one way only.

The office was as she had left it, neat and tidy. If Leigh was true to his word with regard to arrival time, she would be out of here before nine-fifteen. It was going to be difficult explaining her reasons for turning down the job to Mrs Carrington, who was hardly going to be pleased to have a lucrative contract terminated. There was even a possibility that her services might be dispensed with on the grounds of unreliability, although this would be the very first time she had ever let the agency down.

A matter she would have to deal with if and when, Tricia told herself firmly. Staying on here, feeling the way she felt, was impossible.

She was in the inner office, having taken through the mail, when Leigh arrived. Ten minutes early, she noted, glancing at her watch. She steeled herself to meet the grey eyes as he came across to the desk, very much aware of his lean attraction in the dark blue suit.

'Before we start,' he said crisply, 'I'd like to get one thing clear between us. Last night's invitation was a courtesy I'd have extended to anyone stuck in town alone at my instigation, be it male, female, old or young. Whatever experiences you may have had in the past, *I'm* not in the habit of asking my secretaries to provide extra-curricular services.'

Tricia's face felt hot. It took all of her control to keep her voice from reflecting her conflicting emotions. 'In which case, it might be advisable to cut out any chance of misunderstanding by keeping the relationship on a strictly businesslike footing,' she responded coolly. 'Inviting me to call you by your first name was hardly that.'

'I've already told you, I don't care for over-formality among those I work in close proximity with.' He put down the briefcase he was carrying with a thud that signified a rapidly deteriorating temper. 'I'll grant that you're an extremely attractive young woman—who'd be even more so with her hair done differently—but there's no shortage. All I want from you is efficiency allied to a little common cordiality. Is that too much to ask?'

Put the way he'd just put it, it all sounded so plausible, Tricia thought wryly. It *was* plausible.

'I think it might be better if you found someone else to take Barbara's place this next month,' she said. 'If you contact Profiles right away, I'm sure they'll have a suitable replacement here this morning. The travel arrangements are already taken care of, so you won't be losing out on time.'

Leigh studied her in silence for a lengthy moment, brows drawn together, eyes narrowed. 'You're really serious about this, aren't you?'

Tricia inclined her head. 'I wouldn't be saying it if I weren't. I don't think we're what you'd call compatible, Mr Smith.'

His laugh was short. 'Then we'll have to agree to differ, because I'm not letting you go.'

'You can hardly stop me from leaving,' she flashed.

'Not physically,' he agreed. 'What I can do is make sure you never get another job through Profiles again if you walk out on me now. They can't afford to lose client trust by using unreliable staff.'

Tricia stared back at him nonplussed. She hadn't anticipated this reaction. 'Surely,' she began, 'it would be better all round if——'

'It would be better all round if we forgot the whole thing and just got on with the job,' came the flat statement. 'I'd like a coffee for starters. I've already a backlog of letters to dictate, plus whatever comes from this morning's batch. Then there's the monthly board meeting at eleven. As Barbara's stand-in, you'll take the minutes. I'm booked for lunch at one, and I have a couple of appointments this afternoon. Check the diary, will you?'

He was moving as he spoke, coming round behind the desk to start leafing through the ready-opened mail she had shortly before placed there. Tricia stood irresolute within touching distance of one blue-clad arm, trying to nerve herself to defy him. The threat to discredit her with the bureau had not been an idle one. He was just about ruthless enough to carry it through.

There were other secretarial agencies, of course, but word tended to get around. She could well find herself out on a cold bare limb when it came to future jobs. Dared she risk that for the sake of her present peace of mind?

Leigh glanced round when she failed to either move or speak. His mouth was sardonic. 'Coffee?'

Tricia forced herself to action. If there had been a time for defiance it was past and gone. She was stuck with the situation and had to make the best of it.

Which wasn't going to be any easier after all she had said. Leigh's whole attitude towards her had undergone a significant alteration. He didn't need to tell her that keeping her on at all was a matter of necessity, not desire. She had managed to thoroughly alienate him.

He was seated at the desk studying one of the letters received when she took the coffee through some several minutes later. He nodded acknowledgement without looking up as she placed the cup with her usual concern for accidental spillage.

'Bring your book through in ten minutes,' he instructed crisply. 'I'll want everything ready for signing before lunch.'

Board meeting or no, Tricia gathered. A regular slave-driver, Pauline had called him. There had been little enough evidence of it yesterday, but he was more than making up for the lack today. Not entirely due to their contretemps, she was sure. This was Leigh Smith at work.

He finished dictating at ten o'clock, leaving her just the bare hour to transcribe twelve pages of shorthand and print out the letters ready for signing. Leigh gave the sheets a cursory inspection before appending his signature to the bottom of each and returning them to her for posting. If she had anticipated any acknowledgement of her speed and accuracy, she would have been disappointed, thought Tricia drily, although he wasn't the first, by any means, to take such matters for granted. She was beginning to dislike the man with an intensity equal to the love she had once felt for him.

Only it hadn't really been love, had it? One couldn't love a man one scarcely knew. Infatuation would be closer to the mark. He had swept her off her feet—taken advantage of an inexperience that must have been obvious to a seasoned man-of-the-world such as he had been even then. If she hadn't been prescribed a course of the Pill for purely regulatory reasons, he might well have made her pregnant: he certainly hadn't given that possibility a thought!

On the other hand, if she hadn't been on the Pill *she* might well have thought twice before taking the risk herself, came the wry rider. Leigh hadn't exactly raped her; she had been as eager for his lovemaking as he had been to deliver it.

'Was there something else?' he asked, cutting in on her thoughts with an abruptness that made her start. Dark brows lifted as colour tinged her cheeks. 'Miles away, were we?'

She seized on the excuse. 'Sorry, yes. I'll get these into envelopes ready for franking.'

'Fine.' He glanced at his watch, checked the time against the wall clock, then closed the file he had been working on. 'We've five minutes to make the board room. The chairman frowns on late-comers.'

Even his own son, Tricia gathered. No filial favouritism here. She wondered briefly if Leigh's mother was still alive, then put the question aside as of no particular importance. So far as she was concerned, the job was all that mattered right now.

The boardroom was a couple of corridors away on the same floor. Panelled in wood on which were hung several excellent landscapes in contrast to the usual complement of boring portrait studies, and solidly furnished with long mahogany table and chairs, it also boasted two fine windows draped and swagged in apricot silk. A long sideboard held silver trays ready set with coffee-cups and plates of biscuits.

All ten directors of the company were present when the chairman took his place on the hour. Adam Smith was in his late fifties, with dark hair shot through with silver. The resemblance between father and son was there in the bone-structure, though the older mouth lacked the younger's cynical edge in Tricia's view. A rather more tolerant character all round, she judged, despite what Leigh had said earlier.

Before opening proceedings, he took the time and trouble to enquire after Barbara Graham's condition, following it up with an informal welcome to Tricia herself as stand-in. Altogether the kind of company principal she had a lot of time for, she reflected as the agenda was read out and matters got under way. Many saw secretarial staff as mere robots.

Coffee was brought in at half-past eleven by one of the restaurant staff, and drunk without any halt in proceedings. Tricia could find no fault with Leigh's performance when it came to outlining plans for a recent acquisition in the shape of a further Swiss electronics company. He was both lucid and concise.

They were finished by one o'clock. With a notebook half filled, Tricia faced an afternoon's hard work. Leigh vanished along with the rest to the director's dining-room, leaving her to return to the office and contemplate a choice between the staff restaurant and a sandwich right here. The thought of the loaf going stale in the refrigerator decided her. She hated waste of any kind.

It was at least peaceful in here alone after the hard-pressed scribbling of the last couple of hours. She could well afford to relax for a while and enjoy both sandwich and a cup of freshly made coffee. The view from the window was superb: she could see down river to Tower Bridge, while St Paul's looked almost close enough to touch.

Basking in sunlight, the city invited exploration. In two years of daily commuting she had never really found the time to do very much sightseeing. She might fit in a little tourist activity herself after work. It would all depend on what Leigh had lined up for her after she finished transcribing the minutes.

She had finished the sandwich and was on her second cup of coffee when the outer door opened to admit a tall, fair-haired man who paused on the threshold to afford her a detailed appraisal.

'I guessed the looks, but not the colouring,' he announced with an appealing grin. 'I'd have said a redhead.' He came across to offer a friendly hand. 'I'm James Bryant. We spoke on the phone yesterday.'

Tricia shook the hand and answered the smile, responding both to his easy manner and his somewhat rakish good looks. 'Sorry to disappoint you, Mr Bryant.'

'Who said I was disappointed? Brunette is even better.' He studied her for a brief moment with his head on one side and a contemplative expression in his blue eyes. 'Not too keen on the hairstyle, though. It doesn't do you justice.'

'Sorry about that too.' Tricia kept her voice deliberately light. 'I'm afraid Mr Smith is still at lunch.'

'It isn't Leigh I came to see.' The grin came again. 'I was intrigued enough by what he said about you to want to see for myself.'

'What exactly *did* he say?' The words came out sharper than she had intended, causing her to bite her lip and modify her tone. 'Or is this just some kind of joke at his expense?'

'Now where would be the point in that?' He perched on the edge of her desk, smile teasing rather than taunting. 'He said you were efficient, attractive, and more uptight than any woman he'd ever met before. Would *you* say that was an accurate summing-up?'

Tricia felt composure desert her. She said tautly, 'That would depend on what's meant by uptight. If it's "unreceptive to personal overtures" I'd go along with it.'

Speculation sprang in the blue eyes. 'Been indulging in a little harassment already, has he?'

The word alone was enough to pull her up short. She hadn't meant to say what she just had. Whatever remarks Leigh had made about her, it wasn't important enough to get in a spin about. He was entitled to his opinion.

'That's not a phrase I bandy about,' she responded. 'And I'd be grateful if you didn't either. Mr Smith and I don't see eye to eye, that's all.'

'Something of a novelty for him. In Barbara's eyes, he can do no wrong.'

Barbara, thought Tricia drily, didn't have the same basis to work on. Aloud she said, 'The difference between permanent and temporary perhaps. Is there any message I can take for you, Mr Bryant?'

'The name,' he returned, 'is James. No message. As I said, I came to see you. I understand you're staying in town this week. How about dinner tonight?'

Tricia had to smile. There was something very appealing about his easy manner. 'You don't believe in wasting any time, do you?'

'Life's too short,' he agreed. 'I came, I saw, I was conquered! I'm going to be needing a new secretary myself in a couple of months. My present one is leaving to take up motherhood as a career. We could discuss it by candle-light.'

'I don't take permanent posts,' Tricia responded. 'And I'm quite sure there must be several candidates already available in your company.'

'None I fancy sharing an office with on a regular basis.' He studied her for a moment in silence, a curious expression in the blue eyes. 'Why the dislike of permanent jobs? There's no security in temping.'

Tricia lifted her shoulders in a brief shrug. 'It suits me.'

'Fair enough.' James was obviously not about to press the issue. 'Back to tonight. Pick you up at eight?'

About to answer, Tricia let the words die on her lips as the door opened again. Leigh gave the two of them a comprehensive scrutiny, mouth twisting as his eyes came to rest on the man still seated on the desk-edge. 'Looking for me?'

'Not so as you'd notice,' answered the other imperturbably. 'I just asked Tricia to have dinner with me tonight. No objection, have you?'

'I'm afraid I already have an engagement tonight,' lied Tricia on impulse before Leigh could answer. 'But thanks all the same.'

'Too bad.' It was obvious from James's tone that he didn't believe her, although he looked philosophical about it. 'How about tomorrow night?'

'We'll be working late tomorrow night,' said Leigh. 'And for the rest of the week. I want everything cleared before we leave on Monday.' He was moving as he spoke, making for his own door. 'See you, James.'

Tricia kept her face carefully composed as she looked at the man now standing again. 'Sorry.'

'So am I,' he said wryly. 'Maybe we could get together after you get back from Europe?'

'That would be nice.' She switched on the computer, poising her fingers over the keys as the VDU came to life. 'I'd better get on.'

'Don't let him work you too hard,' James advised. 'He takes a mean advantage at times. Bye for now.'

Alone again, Tricia wondered if she might have responded more favourably to the invitation if Leigh hadn't chosen that moment to walk in the door. James Bryant had offered the kind of light-hearted companionship she could do with right now.

The thought of doing overtime for the rest of the week wouldn't normally have fazed her; it was the fact that she would be working late with Leigh. If she was to get through the coming weeks without cracking up, she had to put all personal feelings aside and concentrate solely on the job itself. It was the only way.

Heathrow on a Monday morning was busier even than Tricia had anticipated. She checked in for the flight immediately on arrival, and was dispatched to the airline's first-class lounge to await Leigh's coming.

Seated, with a coffee to hand and a magazine in her lap, she tried to relax and view the coming trip with detachment. Three more weeks, hopefully no more than that, and she could turn her back on Leigh Smith for the last time. She could hardly wait for the day to come.

These last few days had been a trial in themselves. True to his word, he had kept her at her desk until gone eight each evening. His attitude towards her had remained at all times cool and businesslike, with the strain entirely on her side. Whether he had recognised it she had no way of knowing. If he had, he would probably have put it down to resentment over his forcing her to see the job through.

'Good morning,' said the subject of her thoughts, dropping into a seat at her side. 'Have you been here long?'

Tricia adopted the same casual tone to answer. 'About half an hour. I always allow more time than I need to go anywhere in case of hold-ups.'

'A good policy.'

'Not always,' she confessed. 'I've sometimes spent twenty minutes or more driving around the block in order not to arrive too early for a dinner invitation. There's nothing worse than having the doorbell ring at seven-fifteen when the invite said seven-thirty for eight.'

'I can think of several things worse,' Leigh returned drily, 'but I take your point. I'll have coffee too,' he added to the stewardess hovering at his elbow. 'Black, please.'

The girl smiled. 'Of course, Mr Smith. Nice to see you again.'

He returned the smile. 'Nice to be recognised.'

Watching the other face, Tricia thought it likely that *his* was indelibly imprinted on her memory from previous journeys made. Wearing a pale grey suit with a self-striped white shirt and silver-grey tie, he made the darker-suited men in the lounge look dull and provincial. Her own choice of navy blue skirt and matching jacket suddenly felt it. She was glad that she had packed her customary variety of outfits. Travelling light might be a virtue to some, but it limited one's options. She was still hoping for the opportunity to do a little sight-seeing in the evenings. At this time of year it wasn't going to be fully dark until around ten o'clock.

As if sensing her regard, Leigh turned his head to look at her, one dark brow lifting a fraction. Tricia made herself hold his gaze, but could do nothing about the warmth she could feel creeping under her skin.

'You're obviously a regular patron of the line,' she said in an effort to cover her discomposure. 'How many times a year do you make this tour?'

'Twice,' he acknowledged. 'But I use the same line on private trips too. I usually spend a week or so skiing at Klosters in February, then take a break somewhere warmer during the summer. The company yacht comes in useful. Do you like the sea yourself?'

Her heart jerked; she was surprised to hear her voice sound so even. 'I never did any small-craft sailing.'

Leigh looked amused. 'I'd hardly call an eighty-footer that small. She's motorised, not sail. Used for entertaining clients or as a perk for executive staff. She's berthed at Antibes.'

'How the other half lives!' commented Tricia lightly. 'You do your employees proud.'

'The company does. I'm as much an employee as anyone.'

'With rather more power than most, I should have thought.'

'There are nine other directors,' he pointed out.

'Not all of them sons of the chairman, though. Not that I'm suggesting any nepotism,' she added hastily. 'I'm sure you got where you are on merit.'

'Thanks.' The sarcasm was mild. 'You wouldn't be the first to doubt it.'

A waste of time denying the inference any further, Tricia decided. She wasn't even sure she wanted to deny it. Leigh was a more than competent MD, there was no doubt, but it was unlikely that he would have made it this far at thirty-five without a little leverage.

The coffee came along with the call to board. Leigh made no particular effort to hurry, draining the cup before finally getting to his feet. The stewardess who welcomed the two of them on to the plane also called him by name. They had seats on the front row, with all the leg-room even someone of Leigh's height could want. Luxury with a capital L, Tricia thought, relaxing in cushioned comfort. Flying economy after this would be a real come-down.

With the flight scheduled to arrive at midday local time, snacks only were served en route. Not that the trays of canapés and delicate smoked salmon sandwiches left anything to be desired in Tricia's view. Sipping champagne along with the elevenses, she felt like royalty.

Money might not be everything, but it certainly made life agreeable.

Leigh refused food, though wasn't averse to the champagne. Since boarding, his conversational overtures had been limited, his attention given to the file he had taken from his briefcase. A résumé of the Dutch branch's performance over the past six months, Tricia guessed, resisting the temptation to glance over his shoulder. She could only hope for their sake that it was up to scratch.

In seats as wide as these, there was none of the shoulder-rubbing almost inevitable back in economy. On a longer flight, the reclining position would make sleep fairly easy to come by, she reckoned. One or two people were taking advantage of the opportunity regardless. For herself, the very thought of dozing in public was offputting. The man across the aisle, whose mouth had fallen open, looked half-witted.

They landed at twelve on the dot, went through baggage reclaim and Customs without too much of a wait, and were met in the arrivals hall by a blond-haired man in his forties whom Leigh introduced as Paul Munster, general manager of the Netherlands contingency.

Taking the hand held out to her, Tricia said smoothly, '*Aangenaam, mijnheer.*'

The man looked first surprised, then gratified. 'As I am glad to meet you too, Miss Barton,' he replied in excellent English. 'It isn't often that we hear our own language spoken.'

Tricia laughed. 'Don't credit me with any great linguistic ability. I read up a few simple phrases for politeness's sake, that's all.'

'But the thought was there, which is what counts.' He seized both suitcases, and indicated the exit doors. 'I have a car waiting.'

'Efficient *and* thoughtful,' commented Leigh as the other man moved ahead of them. 'A rare combination!'

There was no perceptible satire in his tone, but no doubt, Tricia thought, it would be there in the line of his mouth. 'A little effort never hurt anyone,' she returned levelly. 'In case you're wondering, I also learned the same few phrases in German.'

'It wouldn't have occurred to me to doubt it,' he said. 'I can see you're going to prove an even greater asset on this trip than I anticipated.'

'On a par with Barbara?' she enquired lightly, and sensed rather than saw his faint smile.

'I'll reserve *that* judgement until later. We have a long way to go.'

Don't read innuendo into that statement, Tricia warned herself. He simply meant what he said. Five countries in twelve days. If nothing else, it was certainly going to be hectic.

The waiting vehicle was long and sleek and superbly comfortable. Chauffeur-driven too, which gave Paul the opportunity to draw Tricia's attention to points of interest once he discovered that it was her first visit to Amsterdam.

Leigh said little, though he looked relaxed enough. They were to lunch in the executive dining-room, Tricia gathered, with their luggage transferred to their hotel by the chauffeur. Dinner tonight was to be at the GM's own home. His wife, Gerda, Paul said, was looking forward to meeting Leigh again.

The offices of Brinkland Netherlands fronted on to Dam Square, its imposing façade overshadowed by the vast bulk of the Royal Palace at the far end. The statue topping the latter was known as the Virgin of Peace, Paul supplied when asked. Holding the Rod of Mercury in one hand to represent trade, and an olive branch in the other, she signified the city's twin ideals.

Tricia was glad to find the building as architecturally unspoiled inside as out. There had been some modernisation, of course, but done in a way that was unobtrusive. Whisked straight to the top floor via an iron-caged lift, they were shown into a comfortably furnished dining-room where several other of the executive staff awaited their arrival.

Leigh, Tricia noted, addressed everyone present by first name, and was himself accorded the same casual return—an American-type informality she wasn't at all sure she agreed with. Not that there appeared to be any lack of respect. The deference was there all right, simply not over-emphasised.

Temporary or not, as personal secretary to the MD, she found herself afforded the same friendly courtesy. There were solicitous enquiries after Barbara's state of health, and relief expressed when informed that the operation had gone through without incident and convalescence was under way. A considerate top management altogether on the face of it, Tricia reflected—always providing that the same consideration extended to lower staff levels too.

The afternoon was spent visiting all the departments in the company with Paul and his chief accountant. Leigh seemed to take no particular note of the various proceedings, yet his comments at the end revealed a detailed ingestion Tricia could only admire. He was even able to suggest a certain cost-cutting exercise in Dispatch which no one else had apparently thought of. A managing director in every sense, she conceded.

At four-thirty, with Leigh himself the instigator, the two of them were driven to their hotel, from where they would be picked up at eight for dinner.

'A commitment difficult to get out of,' Leigh remarked on the way to their rooms in the lift. 'Good of Paul to arrange it, but I'd have preferred not to.'

'Any particular reason?' asked Tricia, struck by something in his tone, and received an ironic glance.

'You could say that. You and Gerda have a lot in common.'

Her brow wrinkled. 'In what way?'

'You both of you read too much into too little.'

'Oh, I see!' She made no effort to control the sarcasm. 'Another courteous gesture taken the wrong way?'

'Except that in Gerda's case the so-called overture was received in rather different vein.'

Tricia looked at him sharply. 'You're trying to say she actually responded?'

'I'm not *trying* to say anything,' he came back drily. 'Nor did I misread the situation. Gerda is a very beautiful woman with a sex-drive one man obviously doesn't satisfy. Short of some very plain speaking, I found it difficult enough last time to put the record straight.'

'You don't fancy her at all?' Tricia put everything she knew into keeping her tone from reflecting her inner turbulence.

His smile was faint. 'I wouldn't go as far as that. As I said, she's a beautiful woman. Most men would fancy her. Paul is around ten years older than she is, and rather overwhelmed by her.'

'Then you might be doing him a favour by taking her off his hands.'

The lift had come to a halt at their floor. Leigh made no immediate move to exit, eyes hardened to granite as he studied her. 'There are times,' he said grimly, 'when you overstep the mark yourself!'

Tricia was aware of it. The remark had been, at the very least, thoroughly tasteless.

'I apologise,' she said stiffly.

'Accepted.' The granite was still there. 'A cold shower might do us both good.'

The rooms were adjoining. Once inside hers, with the door closed, Tricia leaned her weight against it for a moment to gather herself. The emotion that had shot through her when Leigh talked about Gerda had been jealousy, pure and simple. Against his principles though it might be to indulge himself with the wife of a company employee, he was obviously smitten by her. The coming evening was going to be difficult in more ways than one.

CHAPTER FOUR

REGARDLESS of better judgement, Tricia found herself taking extra care later with her preparations for the dinner party. After her shower, and with Blue Grass body lotion smoothed everywhere she could reach, she touched the matching perfume to her pulse-points before donning lace-trimmed briefs and bra and pulling on the sheer garter-top stockings she had laid out ready.

Normally fairly sparing with make-up, she paid particular attention to her eyes tonight, subtly highlighting their colour with grey-green shadow and dark brown mascara. Her hair caused the most hesitation. Up to now she had worn it up, but it looked too severe for a social event. Down, and brushed to shining obedience, it curved about her face in soft waves. It was shorter by six or eight inches than three years ago, to say nothing of the colour difference, so hardly likely to set any recognition bells ringing.

The dress she had chosen to wear was in dark green crêpe de Chine. High at the neckline at the front, though dropping to a deepish V at the back, it was cut to follow the lines of her figure down to mid-hip, from where the skirt flared. Her legs were good enough to take the shorter length, she knew, especially in the slender-heeled and finely strapped black leather sandals. Apart from her gold watch and bracelet, the only jewellery she wore was a single strand of cultured pearls at her throat and small pearl studs in her ears.

Carrying the silky-textured loose black coat which did double duty as both rain and evening wear, she was on her way to the door when the knock came. Leigh ran a comprehensive and openly approving glance over her as she stood framed in the doorway.

'That,' he declared, 'is more like it! I was afraid you were going to insist on playing the same role out of duty hours, too.'

Tricia lifted delicate eyebrows. 'Role?'

'You don't need it spelling out.' The grey eyes held mockery. 'Shall we go?'

She closed the door with her back turned to him. Her pulse-rate was fast; she could feel the throbbing in her veins. Wearing a cream jacket over dark beige shirt and trousers, he brought back vivid memories of that first evening on board the *Capucine*. He had worn a suit or dinner-jacket other evenings, of course, but no one dressed for dinner the first night out. She remembered the sheer exultation she had felt on entering the restaurant at Leigh's side and seeing the way other women looked at him, then with envy at her. His appeal had in no way diminished over the years.

Waiting for the lift to arrive, she took care to stand well apart from him. She could feel him studying her—sense his faint frown.

'I still have the feeling I've seen you somewhere before,' he remarked. 'Or someone very like you, at least.'

'It's said we all have a double,' Tricia returned on a surprisingly light note. 'I'm sure that must be it.'

The chime announcing the arrival of the lift came as a relief. The last thing she wanted was for Leigh to start trying to recall where and when they might have crossed paths. The fact that they were going to be spending the majority of their time together over the next two weeks could only increase the likelihood of eventual recognition, she knew. She might consider herself totally different from the girl he had known three years ago, but was she in essence? They had been so close, so intimate.

Yes, but only in the physical sense, came the rider to that thought. They had in no way plumbed each other's depths. What she had to do was continue to stay aloof from him, difficult though that might prove to be. She couldn't bear for him to realise what an out-and-out little fool she had been in the past.

The Munsters' home was alongside the Herengracht, one of Amsterdam's three main canals. Four storeys high and no more than thirty feet in width, the *grachtenhuizen* nestled among others of similar dimensions but totally different character. No two gables were exactly alike, some stepped, some spouted, others constructed in the shape of a bell, all embellished to suit the taste of the individual architect.

Many had the traditional wooden hoist beam jutting from the front, via which larger items of furniture could be hauled to window level at the appropriate floor. Viewing the steep and narrow staircase leading from the equally narrow hallway, Tricia could well appreciate the necessity for alternative access.

Paul greeted them warmly, and took them straight up to the next floor where his wife awaited them in a pleasantly furnished living-room. Gerda Munster was in her mid-thirties, Tricia reckoned from what Leigh had said, but could have passed for late twenties. Blonde, beautiful, and totally sure of herself, she greeted them in English equally as excellent as Paul's, treating Leigh to a smile that suggested a shared understanding.

'It's so good to see you again,' she purred. 'It's been so long since you were last here.'

'All of six months,' he agreed with a dry inflexion apparently lost on her.

'And you are here in Barbara's place,' she said to Tricia. 'Poor Barbara! It's bad enough that she suffer the trauma of an operation!'

Without having a stranger taking over her job, Tricia surmised she meant. She said levelly, 'It's purely a temporary arrangement, of course. Barbara should be back in harness inside the month. A pity, I agree, that she had to miss out on this trip.'

'Yes, she and I are very good friends.' Gerda sounded complacent about it. 'A very nice woman.'

And no threat, reflected Tricia, reading between the lines. Well, neither was she. It was entirely up to Leigh himself to put her off—if that was what he truly wanted.

Dinner was served on the hour with an efficiency Tricia had to admire. Decorated with a superbly executed floral arrangement and sparkling with silver and crystal, the table looked like something out of a magazine.

Gerda herself was the perfect hostess. She preferred, she said, to do her own cooking, although she had a daily housekeeper to keep everything else in order. Looking at the long red talons curved around the delicate wine glass, Tricia could appreciate her lack of enthusiasm for the more mundane tasks.

The woman concentrated the majority of her attention on Leigh, who was seated on her right. If Paul noted her enthralment, he gave no sign of minding. He was an interesting conversationalist, Tricia found, with a sense of humour that sparked a like response. Several times she found herself laughing out loud at some comment.

They finished the meal with coffee and liqueurs back in the living-room. Like everything else Gerda did, she made excellent coffee, Tricia conceded. Perfect hostess though she undoubtedly was, however, the Dutch woman set her teeth on edge.

The way in which she sat rubbing thighs with Leigh on the sofa was too deliberate to be innocent. There might well be something in what he had said earlier— although that didn't rule out the probability of previous encouragement. Blonde, beautiful and twenty-something, had been Pauline's summing-up of his known taste in women. Gerda lost out on one count, but more than made up for it on the others.

Jealousy had a lot to do with the way she was feeling, Tricia acknowledged reluctantly. For three whole weeks she had been the only woman in Leigh's life. Seeing him now, making no attempt to distance himself from the other's overtures, she could imagine how many there had been since. Married or unmarried, it would make little difference to a man of his type.

All the same, it was Leigh who made the first move towards ending the evening. With several meetings scheduled for tomorrow, a reasonably early retirement was a good idea all round, he said firmly when Gerda protested.

'So why don't the four of us visit a nightclub tomorrow night?' she suggested, on realising he was adamant.

'I'm afraid I already made other arrangements,' he responded on a note of regret. 'Perhaps next time?'

'Perhaps.' Gerda made little attempt to conceal her chagrin. The glance she sent Tricia's way was less than friendly. 'I don't suppose we shall meet again.'

'I don't imagine we will,' Tricia agreed. 'Thank you for a very pleasant evening, and a truly superb dinner!'

The flicker of gratification lasted no more than a moment. 'I'm so glad you enjoyed it.'

Leigh had turned down Paul's offer to drive them back to their hotel, and called for a taxi. Seated at his side in the rear of the darkened cab, Tricia made every effort to keep as much space as possible between them. The silence was tangible; she could think of nothing to say in order to break it.

'Tired?' asked Leigh softly after what seemed like an age. 'You're very quiet.'

Emotional tension shortened her tone. 'I'm fine, thanks.'

'Just remarkably bad-tempered.' He sounded suddenly brusque himself. 'What you need is a short, sharp shock!'

About to supply a short, sharp answer, Tricia made a grab at the hand-rail as their driver took a corner without noticeably reducing speed, missed, and found herself thrown bodily against Leigh. 'Like this, you mean?' she asked in an effort to make light of the electric contact.

'No,' he returned sardonically. 'Like this...'

The pressure of his lips on hers took her breath away. For a moment or two, with the memories flooding back, she was powerless to resist, her lips moving beneath his in ardent response. Only when she felt his arm slide around her to draw her closer, felt the hardness of his chest against her breasts, did she come to her senses and tear herself away from him, jerking back into her corner with every nerve-ending in her body on fire.

'Don't do that!' she gritted between clenched teeth. 'I'm here purely as a secretary, not one of your conquests. I thought I'd made that clear enough the other night!'

'The only thing you made clear the other night was the fact that you've been badly enough hurt in the past to make you wary of men wholesale,' he said, inciting a swift and acrid response.

'Oh, so you're a psychologist too!'

'It doesn't take much working out. You were on your guard from the moment we met.' The lean features were bronzed by the passing street-lamps, skin taut over hard male cheekbones. 'The attraction was mutual, but you wouldn't let yourself acknowledge it—any more than you're acknowledging it right now. Just for a moment back there you forgot yourself enough to let go and be a full woman again.'

'Don't mistake shock for endorsement,' Tricia countered. 'I've no intention of joining your list of has-beens, *Mr* Smith.'

'You're already on it,' he said. 'I know who you are— or should I say were?'

This time the shock was total. She sat gazing at him in stunned silence, unable to collect her thoughts sufficiently to even try denying the allegation. 'How?' she whispered without volition, ruling out any chance at all of repudiation.

The strong mouth twisted. 'It wasn't instantaneous, I'll admit. The hair and name alone were enough to throw me off the scent. It was only tonight, when you were laughing with Paul, that it came to me just who you reminded me of. Even then, I wasn't sure until I kissed you just now.'

The taxi driver was listening with an interest that suggested a good enough grasp of the English language for translation. Most Dutch people were bilingual anyway, Tricia reminded herself. She said, low-toned, 'I think we should leave the whole subject alone for the time being.'

Leigh inclined his head. 'We'll discuss it over a nightcap at the hotel. You have a whole lot of explaining to do.'

They completed the journey without speaking again. Huddled into her corner, Tricia gazed blindly out of the window at the bright and busy city streets, and tried to work out exactly what she was going to say when the time came. Not the whole truth, for certain. Leigh must never know how deep her feelings for him had gone. She had to come up with a story that would cover all the salient points, yet still provide adequate concealment. It wasn't going to be easy.

It was barely eleven-thirty when they entered the hotel lobby. Leigh made straight for the residents' lounge, and ordered brandy for them both, sitting back in his chair when it arrived to view her with unreadable expression.

'So?'

'It was just a foolish whim,' Tricia stated, fighting for the nerve to see it through. 'I inherited some money from a relative, and decided to use some of it to see how the wealthy lived for a change. I wasn't born into money.'

'It didn't show.' Leigh's gaze hadn't shifted from her face, eyes penetrating. 'Why the change of name?'

Her shrug was meant to convey wry humour. 'Another foolish whim. It sounded more fitting at the time than my own.'

'As the hair fitted the image better too, I suppose?'

'That's right.' She made herself hold the all-too-seeing regard. 'Blondes have more fun.'

'And that was all you were out for?'

She used the shrug again. 'What else?'

'It was certainly the impression you gave at the time,' he said. 'I had you down for the bored daughter of wealthy parents who'd given you everything except attention. As an act, it was a good one. You could have missed your true vocation.'

The irony stung her into ill-considered retort. 'I'd have scarcely attracted *your* attention as a shrinking violet!'

'True.' Leigh was unmoved by the sarcasm. 'I saw a lovely, sexy young blonde in obvious need of a man. Few could fail to be stirred by that combination.'

'If it was *that* obvious, why didn't you try your luck sooner?' she flashed back, and saw his mouth take on a slant.

'In normal circumstances I would have, believe me. Unfortunately, the virus I'd been suffering from had left me debilitated in more ways than one. The last thing my ego needed was failure. You'll never know what a relief it was to have performance restored.'

'Gratifying to know I was the one to restore it.' Tricia was fighting to retain control of her emotions. Eyes emerald-bright, she viewed him with loathing in her heart. 'It was all a long time ago anyway. I'd prefer to forget about it.'

'If that were true, you'd have turned tail and walked out on this job the moment you realised who I was,' he said. 'You *did* realise, I take it?'

For a brief moment, she contemplated denying immediate recognition, but pride forbade any further subterfuge. 'I realised, yes,' she acknowledged. 'But not until I actually saw you. Smith, after all, is a very common name.'

The dig failed to find its mark. Leigh simply inclined his head in mocking agreement. 'It must have been quite a shock. Which brings us back to the same question. Why did you stay on?'

'Because it was an excellent job, and I saw no reason to let something that happened three years ago stand in the way.'

'Plus you reckoned *I'd* never recognise *you*?'

She said shortly, 'It didn't occur to me that you'd even remember the incident.'

'Rather more than just an incident. We made quite a team those three weeks.'

The memory of it alone was enough to tense her stomach muscles. She made a supreme effort to keep her face from reflecting anything of her thoughts. 'But the season ended, and we each went our own way. It's in the past, Leigh. Let's leave it there.'

He regarded her with an unfathomable expression in his eyes. 'That's the first time you've called me by name since we met up again. Purely reflexive, of course. You've gone to great pains to ward off any kind of familiarity. What happened to you during the last three years to make you so distrustful of motivation?'

'That,' Tricia returned tautly, 'is my business!' She put a hand on the arm of her chair preparatory to rising, looking across at him with veiled green eyes. 'I think we covered all the relevant points.'

'Not by a mile,' he returned equably, 'but we'll leave it at that for now. You didn't drink your brandy.'

'I didn't want it in the first place,' she said. 'You have it.'

'I might at that,' he agreed. 'Not advocated as a remedy for shock, I believe, but a good sleep-inducer. I've a feeling I'm going to need it.'

She was the one who was going to find sleep difficult to come by, reflected Tricia painfully as she left him sitting there. No matter how much she told herself he wasn't worth a second thought, her physical responses still held the upper hand. Not love, not infatuation, but sheer unadulterated desire; that was what he aroused in her. There had been no man before him, and no man since, because she hadn't met anyone else who could make her feel that same totality of need.

Lying in bed some twenty minutes later, she heard the door close in the next room, followed shortly by the sound of rushing water. Showering off the effects of two large brandies, perhaps—or could it possibly be that he was suffering the same frustration that was keeping her awake?

Her whole body ached with longing for his so well remembered caresses, her breasts full and tingling, nipples painfully tensed. She had never indulged in self-relief, and couldn't bring herself to do so now—not because she found the act itself unpalatable, but because it was no real substitute for the ecstasy Leigh's touch had provided.

She slept eventually, of course, but it was a fitful sleep beset by vivid dreams that left her feeling drained rather than refreshed. Viewing the dark circles under her eyes in the bathroom mirror next morning, she reached wryly for her cover-stick, blending in the tinted cream to hide the ravages.

She couldn't afford to have Leigh guess how he affected her still. Not if she wanted to emerge from this whole episode with pride intact. He had made it clear enough last night when he kissed her that he still found her desirable, regardless of changes in appearance. Only it went no further than that, for certain.

He was already seated at a table for two when she went down to the restaurant. Breakfast was a buffet meal, with a choice from a wide variety of both hot and cold dishes. Tricia took a helping of fresh orange and grape-fruit slices, sliding into her seat with a crisp, 'Good morning,' to the man opposite.

'Had a good night?' he asked. 'You don't look particularly well rested.'

'A gentleman wouldn't mention it,' she retorted coolly. 'I'm never at my best after a night in a strange bed.'

She realised what she had said the moment the words left her lips, but it was too late then to retract. She had to force herself to look up and meet the grey eyes. 'A slip of the tongue is no slip of the mind,' she asserted.

'I'll take your word for it.' Leigh sounded amused. 'You'll be meeting up with several more strange beds before this trip is over. It's to be hoped you adjust, or you're going to finish up exhausted.'

'I'll still manage my job, so you don't need worry about that,' Tricia responded smartly, and saw his mouth tilt.

'I'm sure you will. You turned into a real Miss Efficiency!'

'Meaning I was a scatter-brain when you knew me before?'

'Meaning no such thing, and you know it. You've matured in more ways than just age, Emma.'

'Don't call me that!' She caught his change of expression and bit her lip. 'Please,' she added stiffly.

'That's better,' he said. 'I can hardly have my secretary sounding off at me like a fishwife. A slip of the tongue, I think you called it. It can happen to anyone. As a matter-of-fact, I much prefer Tricia as a name.'

'How nice for you.' She made no attempt to curb the sarcasm. 'I prefer Miss Barton myself.'

'Something else that should have clicked earlier, I suppose,' he remarked, ignoring the cutting tone. 'On the other hand, I believe I only heard your surname the once when we first introduced ourselves, so it's hardly surprising that it didn't register.'

What *was* surprising was the fact that he remembered her at all, thought Tricia. By all accounts, he scarcely lived the life of a monk, and all cats looked alike in the dark!

She had acquired a whole new line of cynicism this past week, she acknowledged wryly at that point. So he had remembered. What difference did it make? They were three years, and a whole world apart. Come Barbara's return, that would be the end of it.

'Penny for them?' said Leigh softly.

Green eyes met grey with scarcely a flicker. 'I'd have expected a little more originality from someone of your intellect. Not that I'd have been prepared to let you in on them anyway. My thoughts are private.'

Tolerance gave way to exasperation. 'You're determined not to give an inch, aren't you? Are you going to spend the rest of your life this way?'

'More uptight than any other woman you ever met?' Her laugh sounded brittle. 'That *was* what you told James Bryant, wasn't it?'

'It might have been. It's certainly true enough.' He added with irony. 'You don't appear to have any objection to using *his* first name.'

'I don't work for him.' Tricia dug her spoon into her fruit. 'You've a board meeting in an hour.'

'One of the perks of being boss man is a flexible timetable.' He paused. 'A word of warning if you're thinking of loosening up with James when we get back. He's a great guy, but something of a philanderer. I wouldn't want to see you get hurt again.'

Tricia kept her eyes down. 'It takes one to know one,' she said between her teeth.

One lean brown hand snaked across the white cloth to fasten on her wrist as she began to lift the spoon, jerking the fruit slice from it back into the dish. The grip was nearly hard enough to hurt.

'I'll only take so much from you,' he said in low but none the less meaningful tones, 'old times' sake, or no! My personal life is my own affair. Clear?'

'As crystal.' His very touch made her tremor inside; she could only hope he didn't feel it too. 'I hold the same attitude concerning mine. You need make no concessions for "old times' sake" where I'm concerned. It's purely a business association.'

Leigh left the hand where it was, although his grasp had relaxed a little. 'From the way you reacted last night in the taxi, you're as far from believing that as I am. We had a whole lot going for us three years ago. I wouldn't mind recapturing some of it.'

Tricia felt an iron band tauten about her chest. It was all she could do to force the words out. 'I'm here as your secretary.'

'A daytime distinction I wouldn't argue with,' he said. 'But there'll be time for relaxation.' He let go of her wrist to reach for his coffee-cup. 'Did you ever visit Berlin before?'

Tricia shook her head, struggling to maintain some semblance of equilibrium. 'The only city on this trip that I *have* visited before is Paris.'

'Then we'll have to take the opportunity to see the sights. We're due in Zurich on Friday, which gives us the weekend free before flying down to Milan on Tuesday morning. We'll have to make the most of it.'

'Not in the way you were intimating a few moments back,' she stated. 'I've no intention of recapturing *anything*!'

The dark head opposite inclined in mocking acknowledgement. 'We'll see.'

Biting her lip, Tricia said stonily, 'If you persist in this attitude I'll leave. I don't want your attentions, Leigh. Can't you get that through your head?'

His shrug was dismissive. 'Seems I might have to. If you've finished, we'll get off.' He eyed the navy blue suit with disfavour as she pushed back her chair preparatory to getting up. 'I'm all for suitable dress during working hours, but dark colours aren't an essential. Don't you have anything lighter with you?'

'Nothing *I'd* consider suitable for work,' Tricia returned with deliberation, eying in turn his own choice of silver-grey. 'I prefer dark colours.'

'To match your outlook on life?' Mouth set in sardonic lines, he signed the billing authority placed at his elbow a few moments before by one of the waiters, then got to his feet. 'The car should be here by now.'

It was. Seated, Tricia was grateful for the protection provided by the central arm, although the middle-aged and impassive chauffeur was hardly the type to go screeching round corners. With the sun already hot and giving promise of even greater heat to come, the navy suit was a little heavy, she was bound to concede. Thankfully, the offices, like this car, were airconditioned, so should present no problem. In any case, she would suffer heatstroke rather than allow Leigh to dictate what she should wear!

The day went through its phases. Lunch was taken in the directors' dining-room again, with discussions going on apace. Tricia took notes where necessary, and resolved to order a typewriter from the hotel business supply service and bring everything up to date this evening. That would effectively put paid to any plans Leigh might have in other directions. Recognition was one thing, renewal quite another. Not for anything was she going to risk that degree of hurt again.

Goodbyes were said around four-thirty. Leigh expressed himself well satisfied with matters in general, leaving Paul looking gratified. Gerda sent her regards, he said, and looked forward to the next time Leigh was over.

'I much enjoyed your company last evening,' he told Tricia. 'Should you consider a change of scene when Barbara returns, there would be little difficulty in finding you a post here.'

It was Tricia's turn for gratification. 'It's worth thinking about,' she said, although she had no intention of taking him up on the offer. 'Thank you, Paul.'

'You made a definite hit there,' commented Leigh in the car on the way back to the hotel. 'Not that Gerda would be quite as ready to put out the welcome mat.'

'He was offering me a job, not a home,' Tricia responded smoothly. 'Gerda hardly comes into it.'

He gave her a sharp glance. 'You're actually considering it?'

'Why not? We're all part and parcel of the European Community now. As Paul said, it would be a change of scene.' She paused, then added with purpose, 'Unless you have some objection to my working for the Brinkland Corporation?'

'Hardly. First-rate secretaries aren't all that thick on the ground these days. I just don't happen to see Amsterdam as your scene, that's all.'

'As you scarcely know me, you're not in any position to make that judgement,' she returned, and bit her lip as she saw his slow smile. 'I was referring to the general, not the biblical sense,' she tagged on coldly, thankful for the glass screen shutting them off from the driver. 'Amsterdam would suit me fine. So would the people.'

'Paul in particular?'

'Don't be ridiculous!' She was incensed by the intimation. 'I've no interest in him that way!'

Leigh inclined his head, mouth curling a little at the corner. 'Just a notion. He's a good-looking man.'

'And married,' she clipped. 'That small fact may not have any bearing for you, but it means strictly "hands off" to me!'

The grey eyes narrowed. 'I'm going to say it one more time. There's nothing going on between Gerda and me.'

'If there isn't, it's not from lack of desire,' she came back recklessly. 'You were both of you all over each other last night!'

'That's so patently untrue, it isn't even worth denying,' he said. 'I don't, however, mind admitting that I wanted you last night—especially on tasting those luscious lips of yours again. The memories kept me awake for hours! That afternoon on the beach in Barbados——'

'Stop it!' Her voice was low and ragged. 'It's all in the past. I'm not even the same person.'

'Yes, you are. No one changes character completely. You've simply learned to act another part, that's all.' He put out a hand and slid it behind her neck, drawing her to him to kiss her lingeringly on the mouth. 'It's still there,' he said softly when he lifted his head again. 'All of it.'

Tricia couldn't deny it. The emotions coursing through her were only too overwhelmingly real. Just one small word would set the whole affair in motion again, only to what end? All Leigh remembered was the physical aspect, because that was as deep as his interest in her had gone, but she would be regenerating so much more. Was it worth the pain that was sure to follow?

CHAPTER FIVE

LEIGH made no effort to hold her as she drew jerkily away from him. Throat aching, Tricia turned her face forward, catching the chauffeur's impassive glance in the driving mirror as she did so. He would probably have shown as little reaction if the two of them had made mad passionate love, she thought. He was paid to drive, not sit in judgement.

'I think it might be best if I went back home,' she said thickly.

'That's out of the question, I'm afraid.' Leigh sounded anything but apologetic about it. 'I need you.'

'Paul could provide a substitute for the rest of the trip, I'm sure.'

'I don't want a substitute.'

'There's such a thing as needs must.'

'There's such a thing,' he returned hardily, 'as keeping one's word. Leave me in the lurch, and I'll do as I said I would the first time you threatened to walk out. I'll also make sure you don't work for Brinkland again in any capacity, so don't imagine you can fall back on Paul's offer.'

Tricia looked back at him helplessly. 'You really would, wouldn't you?'

There was purpose in the set of his mouth. 'I really would.'

'And all for what?'

'That,' he said, 'remains to be seen. The girl I knew three years ago is in there somewhere. If nothing else, it will be interesting to see how long she can stay submerged.'

'For as long as it takes,' she stated, and wished she could feel as assured as she sounded.

They were drawing up before the hotel. Tricia slid from her seat as the commissionaire opened her door and went straight inside to collect her key from the desk. Leigh caught her up at the lifts, looking, she thought, more sardonically amused than annoyed at her peremptory departure.

'We're stuck with each other for another three weeks, at least,' he observed. 'Better accept it. I thought we might take a look at some of the city's attractions, then go on to dinner. Half an hour OK?'

'I was planning on spending the evening typing up the report for file,' Tricia answered as the lift doors opened.

'You can put in some overtime on those after we get back.' Leigh sounded adamant about it. 'There's no great hurry. I like to relax in the evenings on these trips myself.'

'With Barbara?'

'We dine together on occasion, yes.' He gave her an oblique glance. 'And if you're thinking what I think you are, forget it. Barbara's good at her job, and not unattractive, but I don't make a regular habit of bedding my secretaries.'

'Just the temporary ones!' Tricia bit back.

'You're the first temp I've had,' he returned with deliberation. 'Barbara's customary stand-in went into retirement on reaching sixty just a week ago, and hardly offered the same inducement.'

'Perhaps you should insist on vetting the next one,' she suggested.

'Maybe you're right.' They had reached their floor. Leigh put out a swift hand to block the contacts as the doors threatened to close again almost immediately on opening, nodding to her to step through. 'Timing out,' he commented. 'I know the feeling.'

Tricia moved on ahead to her door, and inserted the key in the lock with a surprisingly steady hand.

'Half an hour in the lobby,' said Leigh at her back as he passed on the way to his own door.

Inside the room, she briefly contemplated defying the edict, but had to acknowledge an in-built reluctance. Seeing Amsterdam in Leigh's company had to be better than on her own, and the ball was still in her court when it came to anything beyond that. Let him think her willing to renew their former relationship. It would be some satisfaction to keep him dangling on a string for a while before delivering the final refusal.

With dinner to follow the sightseeing tour, she chose a straight-cut linen dress in pale cream edged around the sleeveless armholes and matching Chanel-style jacket with black braid. Her hair she left down again, only this time brushed back from her face and held in place with a cream and black bandeau.

The eyes gazing back at her from the dressing-mirror as she applied shadow and liner held an almost feverish glitter. Mingled anticipation and apprehension tensed her stomach muscles. Playing the sort of game she was planning with a man of Leigh's temperament was dangerous inasmuch as it could well backfire on her. Perhaps, deep down, what she really wanted was to have the initiative taken from her.

Yet what future could involvement of that nature hold for her? Could she really contemplate going through all that heartache again? Their whole relationship was now, and had been before, of a temporary nature. In a month's time she would be right back to square one.

Self-indulgence, she resolved there and then, was definitely out. She would take what perks Leigh might offer in the way of entertainment, but no way was she going to pay for them in bed! It would do him good to be the one used for a change.

He was already waiting for her when she reached the lobby. Wearing the same jacket and trousers he had worn the previous evening, he eyed her with a certain appreciative amusement.

'Did you bring your whole wardrobe along?' he asked.

'I like change,' Tricia acknowledged, adding almost defensively, 'Any objections to the way I look?'

'Nary a one,' he declared. 'It's a great improvement on the daytime version. Paul himself was moved to remark on the difference last night.'

Her smile was provocative. 'How like men are men!'

There was an answering glint in the grey eyes. 'True. Shall we go?'

Amsterdam was a city of islands connected by hundreds of bridges. A city of narrow streets and gabled houses, of richly decorated towers and churches. It was also a city devoted as much to pedal power as to the internal combustion engine. Some cyclists had child seats at their backs, others carried baskets up front for animal passengers, one or two even trailed a little cart.

The best way of getting around, Leigh confirmed. There was a limit to where motorised traffic could go.

They walked some of the time themselves for the same reason. Passing along one street, Tricia's attention was drawn to an uncurtained window lit, despite the relatively early hour, by a rosy glow from within. The girl who sat reading a magazine was skimpily dressed and heavily made-up, her purpose in being there only too obvious, although she was taking no apparent notice of the passers-by.

'Just a job like any other, that's the way they look at it,' said Leigh easily, noting her sideways glance. 'More financially rewarding, that's all.'

Tricia darted a glance at the lean profile. 'How would you know?'

His smile was fleeting. 'Hearsay. If the time ever came that I had to pay for a woman's company, I'd give the whole thing up!'

She believed him. In his position, and being the man he was, female companionship was unlikely to be in short supply for many years to come. Unless he wanted to spend the rest of his life flitting from one to another, though, there had to come a time when he thought about settling down. As the only son, he surely had to feel some obligation towards furthering the family line? The name itself might be common enough but the bloodline wasn't shared.

Trying to visualise the kind of woman he might consider taking on full time was both difficult and depressing. She would need to be exceptional in every sense. There was a possibility, of course, that he already had someone picked out, and was simply biding his time. Leigh Smith would marry when it suited him to do so, not before. After all, a man's ability to father children went way beyond a woman's to bear them.

They ate dinner at a small and relatively simple restaurant on the Voorburgwal, where Leigh was greeted like a long-lost friend and personally conducted by the proprietor to a table in the window. From this angle the five bridges spanning the canal at measured intervals looked almost as if they were stacked on top of one another, so that a man riding a bicycle across the nearest seemed to be bearing the weight of the next span on his head.

'Interesting optical illusion,' agreed Leigh when Tricia drew his attention to it. 'There are more than a thousand bridges in Amsterdam, so I don't suppose this is the only place where you can see the same thing. It's a photographer's paradise.'

'You've obviously been here many times before,' she said, 'judging from the reception.' The pause was timed. 'Did you ever bring Gerda here?'

Grey eyes took on a definite intolerance. 'For the last time, I'm not involved in any way with Gerda!'

'But you might be if she weren't married to Paul.' It was a statement not a question.

'If she weren't married to Paul it's most unlikely that we'd have met in the first place.' He studied her for a moment, brows lifting. 'Could there be a hint of jealousy in all this?'

Tricia allowed herself a hint of a smile. 'Envy, perhaps. She's very beautiful.'

'And aware of it. I prefer a woman who can accept her looks without constant preening. You're just as beautiful, but in a far more natural way.'

Pleasure brought warm colour to Tricia's cheeks. She laughed to cover her momentary confusion. 'Good fishing merits a good catch!'

'Consider me landed.' Leigh was smiling too. 'What would you like to eat?'

Tricia turned her attention briefly to the menu, which was written in both Dutch and English, then said softly, 'Choose something for me.'

'In that case, we'll both have the vegetable consommé followed by *stokvis*,' he returned. 'That's whitefish cooked in milk.'

'Sounds interesting.' At that precise moment Tricia couldn't have cared less what they ate and drank. Seated here like this across from Leigh it was like going back in time.

They had dined together every evening on board the *Capucine*, and discovered a liking for much the same things. The food had been superb. For the first time in her life she had feasted on lobster and langoustine, on genuine caviare and quail eggs, on mouth-watering desserts such as she had hitherto only seen illustrated in top-flight cookery books. The whole three weeks had been like a dream—from which she had awakened with a jolt that had changed her whole life.

The question was, did she really want to risk that kind of pain again for the sake of paying Leigh out in his own coin? It would be too fatally easy to fall in love with him all over again—and with far more impact than before.

She looked up to find him watching her with a curious expression in his eyes, and fought to conceal any giveaway emotion in her own.

'Tomorrow at this time we'll be in Berlin,' she said somewhat obviously. 'Another first for me.'

'It isn't a city for light-hearted sightseeing,' Leigh returned. 'Still too evocative of the past. But it does have its bright side. Berlin nightlife is among the best in Europe.'

As if aware of her oscillating mood, he steered clear of any personal overtures during the following hour or so. They were halfway through dessert when he was hailed by one of the women in a party being shown to a nearby table.

'Leigh!'

'*Hoe gaat het met U?*' he asked smilingly.

No name, Tricia noted, just a polite 'How are you?', but there was no mistaking that look in the other's eyes. If Gerda Munster was out of bounds so far as Leigh was concerned, this young woman almost certainly hadn't been at some time.

The rest of her party had moved on to their table, the man who appeared to be her present partner looking back with a frown as if only just aware of her absence. The girl pulled a wry face, and said something low-toned before moving on without so much as a glance in Tricia's direction.

'An old friend?' she asked lightly.

'An acquaintance,' Leigh corrected. 'If the cake is proving too much for you, leave it. The slices were extra large.'

Tricia had already decided that for herself. The last thing she needed was permission to waste the remainder! She was being ridiculous, she knew, but she didn't care. The Dutch girl probably wasn't the only one of Leigh's feminine 'acquaintances' they were going to run into during this trip. No doubt he had them lined up in every city!

The risk of falling again for a man she knew to be a born philanderer was minimal, she decided. Who would be fool enough? It would give her a whole lot of pleasure to lead *him* up the garden path for a change.

They were back at the hotel by eleven. Going up in the lift, Tricia mentally rehearsed a plea of tiredness to counter the anticipated move towards extending the evening. She framed the words ready for use when Leigh took her key from her to open her door, and was disconcerted to have it handed back to her without even a momentary hesitation.

'We've an early start tomorrow,' he said. 'Breakfast at seven-thirty. Have a good night, Tricia.'

She was aware of a sudden deflation as he moved away, of an unwillingness to let it go at that. She forced herself to step into the room and close the door, standing for a moment to reflect on her thwarted intention. Exactly who, she wondered wryly, was playing with whom?

From arrival at Tegel airport, the day followed much the same pattern as the first. Berlin didn't have too much left to offer in the way of architectural beauty from what Tricia could see of it in passing through, although the grey skies and slanting rain hardly helped, she was bound to admit. After leaving bright warm sunshine, the change was depressing in itself. June was supposed to be one of the best months for weather too.

She found the German contingent easy enough to get along with, if rather formal. The GM here, Karl Heinicke, was a good ten years older than Paul Munster. He appeared to take it for granted that Leigh would prefer to arrange his own evening entertainment.

'A tacit agreement,' the latter confirmed on the way to the hotel when Tricia asked if it was the usual arrangement. He cast her a glance. 'You'd have preferred the personal touch?'

'I wouldn't have anticipated inclusion in any case,' she denied swiftly. 'I'm quite capable of entertaining myself for the evening.'

Leigh lifted an ironic brow. 'Is that supposed to tell me something?'

'No more than it says. You don't have to feel any obligation towards me.'

'Obligation,' he returned, 'doesn't come into it. We're going out on the town, you and I. Dancing, dining, cabaret—anything you fancy.'

She gave him a sideways glance, a deliberated smile. 'Anything?'

'Within reason.' He made no move to touch her, but his regard spoke volumes. 'That's more like the girl I remember.'

Don't count on it, she thought.

Situated smack bang in the centre of town, the hotel was plush, with a gleaming gold foyer to welcome the incoming guest. As before, their rooms were adjoining. Whether the arrangement had been the same when Barbara was accompanying, Tricia had no way of knowing and wasn't about to ask. The communicating doors could only be opened from each individual side, so hardly presented any opportunity for uninvited entry.

With a selection of six or seven outfits from which to choose, she settled on her favourite cream again, this time in a silk shirtwaister which would take her through the evening with the addition of the gold costume jewellery carried in her handbag.

The weather had cleared during the afternoon, making a coat unnecessary. Sunlight put a totally different complexion on things, Tricia acknowledged, viewing the city scene from her window while waiting for Leigh to call for her. They were close to the Tiergarten here—an oasis of woodland and lakes she doubted there would be time or opportunity to explore. But then any sightseeing at all was a bonus.

It was almost five o'clock before the anticipated knock came on the door.

'Sorry to take so long,' Leigh apologised. 'I had a couple of phone calls to make.'

Keeping the home fires burning? wondered Tricia with renewed cynicism. Aloud, she said lightly, 'I was only just ready myself, so perhaps as well. I'd hate to have kept you waiting.'

'You're the only woman I ever knew who would let it worry her,' came the equally light response. 'Not that you wouldn't have been worth waiting for.'

Facile as it was, the compliment warmed her. She would really have to watch it, she told herself. Leigh was too practised in the art of pleasing a woman to be treated with anything but caution.

Situated at the centre of the broad avenue running right through the Tiergarten, the sixty-seven-metre-high Siegessäule offered a superb view over the whole city. The Brandenburg Gate and Reichstag on the eastern edge of the park looked almost within walking distance. No Wall cut off the former from the west now. Modelled on the entrance arch to the Acropolis in Athens, it stood revealed in all its triumphal splendour.

Most points of interest in the city itself were sombre symbols of the war years. Tricia wasn't all that sorry when Leigh suggested they give the general sightseeing a miss and stick to the rural charms of the Tiergarten for the next couple of hours.

They were by no means alone in that preference. The sunshine had brought many more people out to wander the ways. Tourists were here in no small numbers either, judging from the variety of languages overheard in passing, although the English appeared to be in a minority.

'Dedicated to sober reflection for the most part,' Leigh confirmed when she remarked on the lack. He indicated an iron seat at the side of the small lake they were passing. 'Want to take a rest? Those heels of yours weren't really made for walking.'

Tricia had been thinking the same thing, though she wasn't about to admit it. 'I'm not having any problem,' she denied, 'but I don't mind spending a few minutes looking at the view. After all, it's still only a little after six o'clock.'

'The night,' Leigh agreed, 'is young. A pity the shops are closed.'

Tricia laughed. 'I hardly see you traipsing round the stores, anyway!'

'I've done my share,' he said. 'Most men have at some time or other.'

'Dragged along by a woman, you mean? I'd have thought you above being coerced into anything you didn't really want to do.'

'You assume a great deal too much,' came the dry response. 'I'm as willing to make concessions as the next.'

'Always providing there's a worthwhile gain, of course.' Seated, with bare inches between them, Tricia was tinglingly aware of the taut muscularity beneath smooth fawn cloth. 'What *would* you be doing tonight if I weren't with you?'

'What you really mean,' he said, 'is who would I be seeing?' His shoulders lifted. 'I know one or two people who'd be happy enough to join me.'

'Female, of course.' Tricia couldn't quite eradicate the caustic edge.

'Not necessarily.' There was a faint smile on his lips. 'Sometimes I prefer to relax in congenial male company. Tonight, however, isn't one of those times, so you can forget what you were about to say.'

She had been about to say he was perfectly free to seek more congenial company any time he liked, which hardly smacked of originality, she had to admit. 'It hadn't occurred to me,' she lied. 'I'm sure you wouldn't have hesitated to ditch me if you'd wanted to.'

'Which doesn't exactly suggest a very high degree of trust on your side.' He slid an arm along the bench back and drew her towards him, bending his head to put his lips lightly to hers. 'What do I have to do to prove myself?' he murmured against her mouth.

Tricia said thickly, 'Stop it, Leigh. People are watching!'

'A couple kissing on a park bench is no unusual sight even here,' he said, but he released her anyway, sitting back to regard her with an enigmatic expression in his eyes. 'You can't seem to make up your mind what you do want.'

Her heart hammered suddenly and painfully in her ears. 'What's that supposed to mean?'

'It means if you're planning on giving me the run-around, I'd think again. I'm not going to be made the whipping-boy for whoever it was that let you down.'

The irony of it brought a brittle little smile to her lips. 'I never said I *had* been let down.'

'You don't need to say it. Your whole attitude says it for you.' He paused, regard too penetrating for comfort. 'You worked for Alan Parker at Grant-Dawson, didn't you? Was he the one?'

'No!' The denial came out sharper than she had intended, sounding, even to her own ears, over-emphasised. She muted her tone to add, 'I hadn't the slightest interest in Alan Parker as anything but an employer.'

'But you left rather suddenly, and for no good reason, according to their personnel officer.'

Green eyes sharpened. 'You've been asking questions about me?'

'None I wasn't entitled to ask. If it wasn't Parker, why *did* you leave?'

She looked away to where two small children were feeding ducks. 'I already told you, financial gain.'

'Except that I happen to know what you were on at Grants, and can work out what you're probably averaging with Profiles.'

'So I miscalculated a little.' Tricia kept a tight rein on her self-control. 'If I'd had an affair with anyone, it certainly wouldn't have been with a married man!'

Leigh said softly, 'You didn't bother asking me if *I* was married three years ago.'

She tensed. 'That was different.'

'No more than a simple holiday romance, so status immaterial, you mean?'

'Something like that.' The whole conversation had reached a point beyond which she had no wish to go. Voice husky, she added, 'I'd prefer not to be reminded of past indiscretions.'

'You look back on it with regret?' There was a note of wry humour in the question. 'I can't say the same myself. I remember the way you looked in that bikini. You had the most perfect body. Still have, I'd say, although you seem to make a point of keeping it well covered these days. Deliciously uninhibited too. That was the first and only time I ever made love in the sea!'

'Are you deliberately trying to embarrass me?' she demanded, and sensed his smile.

'I'm attempting to find the girl you were then underneath the veneer you've donned since.'

'In the hope of a repeat performance?'

'I'd be a liar to deny it,' he admitted. 'I felt the same spark the moment you walked into the office a week ago, even if I didn't immediately recognise it. You were right to suspect my motives when I asked you out to dinner that evening. It wasn't a move I was in the habit of making at all. You intrigued me to a point where my customary rule regarding personal involvement with an employee went out of the window. As a temp, you were a different proposition, I persuaded myself.'

Tricia couldn't bring herself to look at him directly for fear of what she might give away. 'So all the self-righteous indignation next morning was just so much hot air!'

'You could say that. I'd been given the red light in no uncertain terms; it brought out the bull in me. You were coming on this trip whatever it took!'

'Even blackmail?'

'A harsh term, though fitting, I suppose.' He sounded far from contrite. 'I'd no real intention of acting on the threat.'

'I wasn't to know that,' Tricia pointed out, 'so it was still reprehensible. Especially from a man in your position. Not the kind of behaviour your father would approve of, I'm sure.'

'Does that constitute a threat to tell him?'

There was more quizzical amusement than trepidation in the query. He knew full well, Tricia reflected wryly, that she was only talking for talking's sake.

'I wouldn't even consider it,' she said. 'Neither, if it comes to that, would I consider a re-run of what's past and gone.'

His mouth twisted. 'But you weren't averse to playing me along.'

There was no point in trying to pretend that she didn't know what he was talking about. 'A temporary insanity,' she claimed.

'Which brings us back full circle to the question of motivation.'

'You're like a dog with a bone!' she snapped back, losing what little composure she had managed to retain over the last few minutes. 'I thought you needed taking down a peg or two. Is that motivation enough?'

'Taking it for granted that I'd have let you get away with it. Supposing I'd decided to go further than just opening the door for you last night. What would you have done about it?'

Tricia made every effort to level her voice. 'Told you just where you got off.'

'That might not have worked. In fact, I'd go so far as to say it would have proved downright inflammatory.' The pause was deliberated. 'Maybe that was the reaction you were counting on.'

'Freud reincarnated!' The sarcasm crackled. 'Maybe you should stop trying to analyse me and start work on yourself!'

'No analysis needed,' came the unmoved retort. 'We both basically want the same thing. The only difference being that you don't want to admit it.'

'Think what you like.' She came to her feet, unsurprised to find her limbs shaky. 'I'm going back to the hotel.'

He caught her up before she had gone three yards, falling into step at her side. His face in profile looked austere.

'Do you aim to spend the rest of your life being self-sufficient?' he asked. 'Or is this just a temporary phase?'

'*Que sera sera*,' she retorted with calculated flippancy, and gasped as his hand fastened on her shoulder, dragging her round to face him.

The grey eyes held a purposeful glitter. Tricia made a feeble attempt to avoid his mouth by turning her head away, but he simply seized her by the nape with his free hand and held her firmly in position. The kiss was scorching, arousing a hunger for more. She was incapable of saying a word when he finally let her go, though not too far gone to disregard the indulgent glances and smiles of passers-by.

'You're not going back to the hotel,' he said. 'At least, not yet. We're going to spend the evening the way we planned. Call it part of the job. You said you were prepared to make yourself available whenever needed.'

'This isn't part of the job, and we both know it,' Tricia forced out. 'Leigh——'

He cut her off by the simple expedient of laying two fingers across her lips. 'All right, so I'm asking. Just dinner, if you like. No commitment.'

She was torn between two fires. He might say no commitment, but the more time they spent together, the more difficult it was going to be to contain the desire they were both aware of. Just standing here like this looking up into that lean, hard-boned face made her ache to have his arms about her, his lips on hers again. He had set a precedent no other man she had met could match.

So let it happen, came the tempting thought. At least have that much out of it. She might regret it later, but it was now that mattered. She wouldn't even think about the future!

Leigh relaxed as he saw the change of expression in her eyes. 'That's better,' he said. 'Let's go and find a taxi.'

It was the start of an evening that Tricia enjoyed as much on actual merit as anticipation. They started out with cocktails in one of the city's more up-market café-bars on Hardenbergstrasse, progressing from there to a restaurant in the suburbs which served traditional German food at its best. There was a small dance-floor, with music provided by a pianist playing numbers from the Thirties era.

'Have you been here before?' asked Tricia, enjoying the atmosphere.

'Once or twice,' Leigh acknowledged. 'Not often enough for the name to be recognised.'

The dry humour drew an answering smile to her lips. 'Do you find it a problem at times?'

'It could be worse. My mother favoured John as a first name.'

'Is she still alive?'

'Very much so. She's married to a property tycoon, resident in Switzerland.'

'I'm sorry,' she said quickly. 'I didn't know your parents were divorced.'

'Fourteen years ago.' There was no particular inflexion in his voice. 'It happens.'

Was that part of the reason he had steered clear of marriage himself? Tricia wondered. It wouldn't be from lack of women willing to take on the name of Smith. Given half a chance—— She broke off that train of thought abruptly, aware of his eyes on her and afraid of giving herself away. Marriage certainly wasn't on the agenda.

'Dance?' he asked as the pianist broke into another nostalgic medley.

Tricia nodded and got to her feet, pulses racing as they took to the floor. With several other couples doing the same, it was necessary to stay close. Leigh took her hand and drew it down against his chest, then pressed a light but heart-jerking kiss to her temple.

'Like old times,' he murmured. 'You feel so good, Tricia!'

She felt anything but. Foolhardy would be closer to the mark. Not that she was going to allow it to make any difference. Leigh was irresistible; he always had been. She didn't possess the strength of mind to turn away from him now. Whatever else came of it, she would at least have something to look back on.

CHAPTER SIX

THE hotel was quiet when they eventually got back. Even when they reached their floor, Tricia still wasn't a hundred per cent sure that Leigh's plans ran parallel with her expectations. This time when he took her key from her she found herself praying that he wouldn't be handing it back. She couldn't bear to have him walk away again.

He didn't. Hearing the door close on the two of them, she wondered fleetingly in how many hotel rooms around the world a similar scene was being re-enacted. Not that there was anything sordid about this particular one. What she felt for Leigh went far deeper than mere passing fancy. She had been in love with him three years ago, and she was in love with him now.

He inserted the key back in the door and turned it before touching her in any way. Tricia shuddered when his hands came around her waist to pull her back against him, but it wasn't with dread. She turned her cheek to receive his nuzzled kisses, thrilling to the memory of other nights, other kisses. Whatever heartache was to come it was worth it just to be close again.

Fingers dextrous, Leigh unfastened the buttons down the front of her dress far enough to allow the garment to slide gently to the floor when he eased it from her shoulders, leaving her clad only in lace bra and briefs and sheer stockings. He traced the thin line of her straps down to where they joined the flimsy material, then on over the soft swell of bare flesh until his finger ends met at the hollow of her cleavage and his hands slid below to cup the firm weight of her breasts in the way she re-membered so achingly well.

'Beautiful,' he murmured. 'Utterly beautiful!'

Tricia turned in his arms to lift her face eagerly to his, kissing him feverishly, wantonly, mind blanked off from everything but the desire to be with him again wholly and completely. It was like being brought back to life after years in a semi-coma. She couldn't begin to have enough of him.

Her sheer fervour sparked off a like response. Breathing roughened, Leigh swept her up from the floor and carried her over to the bed, somehow managing to yank back the covers and deposit her on crisp clean linen.

Her shoes had fallen off on the way. Tremor after tremor ran through her as he slowly and carefully rolled down each stocking and drew it from her foot. The only light came from a single orange-shaded lamp in the far corner of the room, which must have been switched on by a maid. It made his skin look like bronze.

He stood up and removed his own clothing before proceeding further. Heart pounding against her ribcage, Tricia watched through slitted eyelids. His body was just as she remembered it: shoulders broad and muscular, chest deep, with a triangle of crisp dark hair, waist narrow, hipline flat and hard. Her breath caught in her throat at the sheer masculine power of him—a Rodin statue come to vibrant life!

There was no self-consciousness in his slow smile as he met her eyes. Too well accustomed to such moments of intimacy, came the fleeting thought, swiftly thrust aside before it could do any harm. It was the here and now that mattered; just the two of them together again.

'You,' Leigh said softly, 'have too many clothes on.'

He sat down on the mattress edge to press a swift kiss to the tip of her nose before sliding his hands behind her back to unfasten the clip of her bra and draw the garment from her. Tricia saw the glow spring in his eyes as he looked at her, felt the pulsing pleasure flood her as the lean hands reached to caress. Her nipples were taut, tingling peaks, jerking a faint cry from her lips at his touch.

She went rigid when he lowered his head to take one tender nub in his mouth. The sensation was almost too exquisite, verging on actual pain. She slid her hands over the broad shoulders to caress the sensitive nerve spot at his nape, allowing him to set the pace. Not that she had a great deal of choice, she fancied. Leigh was in total charge of the whole situation. No doubt he always was.

With briefs so scanty, removal scarcely made any difference. Tricia quivered to the knowledgeable touch, cried out in frenzied abandonment at the peak, welcomed him with wide-spread limbs and passionate response as they came together at last in that so well remembered joining of flesh, of spirit with spirit. Her heart was in it too, whether his was or not.

He said her name at the moment of fulfilment—except that Emma wasn't her name any more. Lying there in his arms with the dark head on her shoulder and his heart thudding against her breast, Tricia tried not to let the slip spoil the moment for her. It had been purely involuntary, she was sure—a momentary back-flip of the mind. She and Emma were one and the same person; why feel any offence?

Because the character she had played three years ago had been quite different from the character she was now, came the answer. If it was Emma he was really looking for, she was no longer there to be found.

'This has to be the most enjoyable European tour I ever made,' he murmured against her neck. 'You're a gift from the gods, Tricia!'

'All part of the service,' she said without consciously forming the words, and felt his lips stop moving against her skin.

He lifted his head slowly to look at her, eyes narrowed a little. 'I hope that was a joke.'

'It was,' she claimed hastily. 'Not much of one, I admit.'

'You can say that again. If I thought——' He broke off, shaking his head and summoning a smile. 'No matter. We all of us say the wrong things at times. I trust you enjoyed it as much as I did?'

Enjoy was too commonplace a word for what *she* had experienced, reflected Tricia, but she had no intention of letting him know that. All he had wanted was a renewal of past pleasures. Having gained his way, he might well lose interest in any further pursuit.

'I hardly need to tell you,' she said. 'You're a superb lover, Leigh!'

An eyebrow lifted in faint sardonicism. 'You consider yourself well qualified to judge?'

'Not from experience, if that's what you mean,' she retorted with asperity. 'I don't sleep around!'

The grey eyes took on a certain wry acknowledgement. 'I'm sure of it. It was a crass remark to make anyway. Making love to you would give any man incentive to surpass himself. You hold nothing back.'

Only her innermost being, she thought, and that would remain hidden.

Leigh rolled to ease his weight from her, taking her with him so that they lay facing each other, bodies still lightly touching all the way down. Tricia resisted the urge to press closer. If he wanted her again she would know it soon enough. For the present it was enough just to be here with him like this, to feel his breath warm on her cheek, the hair on his chest against her breasts, the strength in his thighs.

'There's so much I don't know about you,' he said softly. 'Things I never got round to asking the first time. Not that you'd have given me a straight answer then, I suppose.'

'I had an imaginary background all worked out,' Tricia confessed. 'You weren't far out with the neglected-daughter theme. Looking back, I doubt if it would have stood up to any real probing, though.' She hesitated before tagging on diffidently, 'Lucky you didn't show too much interest at the time.'

'You gave the impression of wanting to remain anonymous,' he said. 'I don't recall you showing much interest in who and what I was either, if it comes to that.' It was his turn to pause. 'So what happened to your real parents?'

'My father was killed in an accident at work when I was a baby, my mother died of cancer when I was sixteen,' she said unemotionally. 'I lived with my god-father's family until I left business training college and got a job that enabled me to be independent.'

'It must have been a bit of a struggle,' Leigh commented quietly.

'More than a bit, but I managed. It got easier as my earning capacity increased, of course, although I never seemed able to afford anything better than a bed-sitter initially. Life on board a cruise liner always seemed the ultimate holiday—probably because it was so unattainable. It proved too much of a temptation when I inherited all that money.'

Leigh kissed her gently on the lips. 'I still don't see why you felt the need for pretence.'

'A kind of inverted snobbery, I suppose,' she admitted. 'I was convinced I'd be ostracised if anyone knew what an outsider I really was.' She attempted a touch of humour. 'If it comes to that, I'm not at all convinced that you'd have paid me the same attention if you'd known the truth yourself.'

He laughed. 'If you'd been a typical dumb blonde I wouldn't have been interested whatever the background. I enjoyed every minute of the time we spent together, not just the lovemaking.'

'But only for the duration,' Tricia said lightly.

'Your choice, not mine—or so I thought at the time,' he replied.

Shaken, she gazed at the face so close to her own, unable to see the expression in his eyes in the dim light. 'What do you mean, *my* choice?'

'You seemed to become withdrawn after Barbados, as if you'd decided it was time to call a halt on the whole affair. For all I knew, you had someone else lined up waiting for you back home. At any rate, I wasn't about to start trying to change your mind.' Leigh's tone was curious. 'Was I wrong?'

An outright yes might well suggest a deeper involvement than she was prepared to have him realise, Tricia thought wryly. She settled for a compromise instead. 'It wasn't so much a lack of interest as the realisation that it had to end anyway once we got back to Southampton.'

'Because you still had me down as the type who'd run a mile once I knew you for what you really were?'

'Something like that.' She stirred restlessly, afraid of giving too much away. 'It's all a long time ago, Leigh.'

'So it is.' He was fully aroused again, reacting instantly to her movement. 'Whereas this is here and now, and more than enough to be going on with.'

Wonderful, yes, but far from enough, she thought, as he came over her once more. Only his love could provide the ultimate fulfilment, and that was as unlikely to be on offer now as it had been back then.

She awoke when he slid from the bed some untold time later, and lay silently watching as he gathered his things and walked unhurriedly to the communicating door. Her side was locked, as she had assumed his would be too. Seeing him open the other door without difficulty, Tricia realised that he had known it would be unlocked, and that could only be because he had done the unlocking himself.

So he had planned in advance for the night to end this way. Had taken it for granted that they would spend at least part of it together. The bedside clock read ten minutes past three, which meant she had been asleep for an hour or so. Leigh must have fallen asleep too, or he would no doubt have left her earlier.

Rolling on to her back, Tricia attempted to rationalise her emotions. She had gone along readily enough, so could hardly lay all the blame at his door. The problem was going to be where they went from here. Was Leigh going to anticipate the same freedom every night? She wanted it herself, she had to admit, though the price would be all that much higher when the time came to part.

She slept eventually, awakening to a vague depression which resolved itself into a full-blown one when memory returned. Showered and dressed, she felt some improvement in emotional control. Nothing that had happened last night committed her to any course of action she didn't want to take. The ball was still in her court.

With no summons from next door, and refusing to take the initiative, she made her way down to the restaurant at eight o'clock. Leigh arrived some five minutes later.

'I tried your room,' he said, taking his seat at the table for two. 'Why didn't you let me know you were ready?'

Veiled green eyes met questioning grey. 'I didn't realise you were expecting a call.'

'No?' A faint line appeared between the dark brows as he studied her. 'I'd have thought it obvious.'

Tricia said carefully, 'I don't expect any special treatment because of last night, Leigh.'

The line deepened. 'What's that supposed to mean?'

'Exactly what it says.' She was struggling to remain cool and collected. 'No commitment.'

'I see.' The grey eyes were suddenly hard as nails. 'Just a one-night stand!'

She winced at the tone. 'What's the alternative?' she demanded. 'A whole string of them! I don't make a habit of sleeping with my boss, temporary or not!'

'So this was as special for you as it was for me.' It was a statement, not a question, the bite gone from his voice. 'I've always steered clear of any personal involvement where it might conflict with business interests—including willing wives of executive staff—but this is different.'

'Because I'm only temporary?'

'That comes into it, if not quite in the way you mean.' Leigh paused, searching her face as if looking for some spark of encouragement. 'When I left you in Southampton it was on the understanding that you weren't interested in anything more than a holiday romance. I appreciate now why you wanted me to think that way, even if I don't agree with your reasoning at the time. What *is* important is the fact that we met up again like this. A second chance, if you like, to get to know one another in more depth. I enjoy your company wholesale, Tricia. I always did. The physical attraction is only a part of it.'

She sat looking at him in silence for a long moment after he finished speaking, unable to convince herself that he wasn't just spinning her a line. Trust was supposed to be an integral part of loving, but she didn't trust him. Not wholly.

'Say *something*,' he urged with a familiar and heart-stirring quirk of an eyebrow. 'Even if it's only get lost!'

Her smile was reluctant. 'I'm hardly in a position to do that.'

'Because you consider yourself under contract?' He shook his head. 'You're free as a bird. If it's your choice to go home, then I won't attempt to stop you.'

She bit down on her lower lip. 'I didn't say I wanted to go home.'

'I know. I was giving you the option.' His voice was soft. 'I'd be a liar if I tried making out that last night was an isolated incident, just as you'd be one yourself if you pretended it was all one-sided. We're as well balanced when it comes to making love as we are on an intelligence level.'

The couple at the next table were hardly close enough to overhear the conversation, Tricia reassured herself, trying to stay on top of her emotions. Leigh sounded so genuine, so plausible—she wanted so badly to believe he was serious in what he was saying. Not that he'd so far given her any real cause to assume that the relationship would continue after this trip was over.

'I think it might be better to just concentrate on business affairs for now,' she said at length. She attempted a laugh. 'My mind can't cope with too much at one time!'

'Your mind,' Leigh declared with irony, 'is capable of coping with anything thrown at it, but have your own way. We've tomorrow to get through with the Zurich people, then a whole weekend to sort ourselves out. I'm willing to put matters on hold till then.'

Including the next two nights? Tricia wondered, and was conscious that relief was not the uppermost emotion. After last night it was going to be more than difficult to stay aloof from the needs Leigh roused in her.

The day was long, though hardly lacking in stimulation. Karl had set up a business luncheon to which Tricia was not invited, leaving her free to join his secretary for a meal in the staff restaurant.

'I do not always eat here,' declared the woman in her precise English when they were seated at the table, 'but today it is convenient. The food is wholesome, yes?'

'Extremely,' Tricia agreed, already over-faced by her choice of *Sauerbraten*, which had turned out to be braised pickled beef. She added conversationally, 'I believe you've been with the company a long time?'

'Fifteen years,' agreed the other. 'The same length of time as Herr Schmidt's regular secretary. We are very compatible.'

Barbara, Tricia reflected, appeared to be on everyone's Christmas list. She must be an extremely nice person as well as good at her job. The thought that in a few weeks' time she would be taking over again brought despondency in its wake. Where she would be herself at that time was very much open to question still.

'You have known Herr Schmidt for some longer time than just these two weeks yourself, I think?' remarked the older woman, jerking her out of her thoughts. There was a certain speculation in the other's regard. 'He is very young to hold such a position. Here in Germany a man is rarely considered to be ready for management at such a level before he is at least forty-five.'

'It isn't all that common in England either,' Tricia returned, disregarding the previous comment. 'But there are exceptions to every rule. Herr Schmidt is well able to handle the job.'

'There is no doubt about that,' Lillian Schneider hastened to assure her. 'He is very highly regarded.' A smile touched her lips. 'Some of the younger female staff consider him very attractive.'

Some of the older element too, Tricia suspected. Lillian was in her early forties, and married, but that hardly ruled her out. Leigh's appeal lay as much in his forceful masculinity as actual looks, and knew no age barriers.

What he might have in mind for this evening, after they finished here, she had no idea. It might even be necessary for them to go their separate ways. That wasn't what she wanted, she had to admit. What she did want was some assurance that it wasn't simply a temporary affair he was after.

She put the problem aside at that point, aware that the other woman was perceptive enough to second-guess the cause of her preoccupation. Whatever the relationship between her and Leigh, it was their business and no one else's.

They were late getting back to the hotel after spending the major part of the afternoon touring a subsidiary factory out in the suburbs. With production figures still falling after major reinvestment in new machinery, Tricia privately saw little hope for recovery, but Leigh was allowing a further six months before recommending any drastic action to the board.

'They'll pull through,' he declared in the car when she tentatively expressed her doubts. 'They just need a little more leeway.' His smile was brief. 'If they don't, it's my neck on the block!'

'You'd hardly be discredited over one error of judgement, I'm sure,' she said, and saw the smile come again.

'What makes you so certain there haven't been others?'

'You wouldn't be where you are if you were given to making mistakes,' Tricia returned promptly. 'If you think they'll make it, they probably will.'

'Only probably? I expect more from you than that.'

She glanced at him swiftly, and away again, feeling her heart thud at the look in the grey yes. No mockery that she could see, just a reflection of her own desire.

'I thought we were going to forget all that until we get to Zurich?' she said low-toned.

'I said I was willing to put it on hold, not out of mind,' came the level reply. 'And I'm not even sure the first is workable. What do you intend doing with yourself this evening?'

'I hadn't considered,' Tricia admitted. 'Dinner followed by an early night, I suppose.'

'I can't think of anything better myself—particularly the early night.'

She said thickly, 'That wasn't what I meant.'

'I know.' His tone had roughened a fraction. 'If I thought you were playing any kind of game with me I'd have had you on that plane this morning. Is dinner together too much to ask?'

'Of course not.' She was already on the verge of telling him nothing was. 'At the hotel?'

'As good a place as any, I suppose. What time is our Zurich flight?'

'Eight o'clock,' she said. 'Arriving at nine-twenty.'

'Then an early night is definitely on schedule. I need to be on top form for tomorrow's meetings. You'd better arrange for a six a.m. call, and breakfast via Room Service.'

Business, Tricia reflected wryly, quite definitely came first. She scarcely knew whether to be glad or sorry that the final decision had been taken out of her hands.

Rather than the feverishly busy city of Tricia's expectations, Zurich had a surprisingly relaxed Mediterranean atmosphere, with pavement cafés and tree-lined streets and picturesque squares. The financiers had to be there somewhere, of course, but they certainly weren't in immediate evidence.

Very little older than Leigh was himself, Ulrich le Tissier revealed a sense of humour that warmed Tricia to him immediately.

The name, he advised over lunch, was the result of having a French-born father and German mother. The latter language was the most widely spoken in Switzerland, with French and Italian in second and third places. Most Swiss people were capable of understanding all three main languages, but would generally talk to each other in Swiss German, which was a language all on its own.

'Thereby endeth the lesson,' he said to Tricia, who was seated next to him, in fluent English. 'You're very good at looking interested.'

'I *am* interested,' she declared. 'I've never been to Switzerland before, and know very little about it. Zurich isn't at all what I expected.'

'Most newcomers hold the same view,' he confirmed. 'Many also believe it to be the capital.'

Tricia laughed. 'I'm not quite *that* unversed. Would you recommend a visit to Berne?'

'I'd recommend that you spend several weeks visiting the country as a whole,' he returned. 'The scenery alone is second to none.' He turned his attention to his British counterpart, who was deep in discussion with one of the other directors. 'You should take the opportunity this weekend to sample a boat trip on the lake, Leigh. The Long Tour goes all the way to Rapperswil and back in just five hours.'

'Sounds attractive,' returned the younger man equably, 'but I already made arrangements to spend the weekend at Winterthur.'

'Ah, yes, of course. You'd naturally wish to visit your mother while you're here.' He turned back to Tricia. 'Perhaps you might like to join my family on Sunday? We live a very casual life at the weekend, but you'd be more than welcome to share it.'

'The arrangement includes Tricia too,' Leigh put in smoothly. 'A well deserved break from duty.'

Considering the amount of work piling up against her arrival back at the London office, she could hardly claim to have been bound to a desk this last week, Tricia reflected. She wondered when the arrangement had been made—or even if it had been made at all. She doubted if Leigh really intended introducing her to his mother.

From the speculative glances cast her way, it was doubtful if anyone else believed the story either. A man travelling with his secretary, a free weekend—it was a standard situation. She did her best to keep her expression from reflecting her inner feelings. Dislike the innuendo though she might, there was little she could do about it. Let them think what they liked!

Sporting five stars, the hotel into which they had been booked was smaller than either of the others, and redolent of an earlier era in its architecture and décor. Luxury and comfort, however, was of the highest order. The rooms themselves were the best yet, Tricia thought, admiring the fine brass bedstead and solid mahogany furnishings.

She went to open the communicating door when Leigh rapped lightly on it, viewing him with an expression that lifted quizzical brows.

'Something wrong?' he asked.

They'd been driven to the hotel in an open car without privacy from the driver, so this was the first opportunity she had had to say what was on her mind. Faced with him now, she found herself floundering a little.

'This weekend,' she said. 'Why did you tell them all we were going to stay with your mother?'

'What I said,' came the unperturbed reply, 'was that we'd be spending the weekend at Winterthur, not necessarily with my mother and her husband. It's a world-famous arts centre, and typically Swiss. You'll like it.'

She studied him nonplussed for a moment. 'You don't intend visiting your mother at all?'

'Hardly. I just don't want to stay at the house, that's all. Her husband and I don't get along all that well. I booked a hotel by phone from Berlin. One of the older ones on the outskirts.'

'What about this place?' she asked. 'There's still Monday night.'

His shrug made light of the matter. 'It'll keep. Do you like opera?'

Thrown by the *non sequitur*, she said blankly, 'Some.'

'How about *Carmen*?'

'One of my favourites,' she admitted. 'But surely you'd need to have booked well in advance to get seats this far into the season?'

'Ulrich has contacts who can fix just about anything. Two tickets for tonight's performance was easy meat.'

'So you already have them in hand,' she said. 'In which case, there was little point in asking my preferences, was there?'

The shrug came again. 'We don't have to use them.'

'Another waste of money—like these rooms going spare over the weekend.'

Leigh looked amused. 'Your concern for company expenditure does you credit. As a matter of fact, the tickets are on Ulrich. A friendly gesture between two people who happen to share similar tastes. He very much approves of you. He said you reminded him of his wife when he first met her. She's English too.' He straightened away from the door-jamb, where he had been leaning a hand. 'We'll eat before the performance. I doubt if I could last the distance without. Half an hour long enough for you?'

'Plenty.' Tricia was past concerning herself with anything beyond the fact that they were going to be together not only this evening but for two whole days and nights to follow. If there had to be doubts they could come later. Her smile was buoyant. 'Half an hour.'

CHAPTER SEVEN

CARMEN was superbly staged and performed. The best production, Tricia acknowledged, that she was ever likely to see and hear.

'The June arts festival is one of the major events in Europe,' agreed Leigh. 'I usually try to coincide my trips with it.'

They had stopped for a drink at one of the pavement café-bars. Sitting there in the balmy night air, Tricia felt at peace with the world. Whatever Leigh had in mind, she was ready to go along.

'Does Barbara like music too?' she asked.

'If that means have I taken her to concerts in the past, the answer is yes,' he responded. 'She's a very cultured woman, and excellent company.' He added levelly, 'Just that, no more.'

'I wasn't suggesting that there might be anything more,' she denied. 'Not that I could complain even if there was. You're a free agent.'

'The same way you are?' His tone hadn't altered, but his mouth had taken on a slant. 'Supposing we forget the temporary business for the time being, and make the most of what time we have? As you've seen so relatively little of Zurich itself up to now, I thought we might spend the morning looking round, then head for Winterthur after lunch. It only takes half an hour by car.'

'Sounds fine to me,' she said, and mentally kicked herself for the unguarded remark. Leigh didn't need telling he was a free agent. 'I can take a look around the town while you visit your mother.'

'You'd prefer not to meet her?'

There was something in the way he said it that drew her eyes, although there was no telling anything from his expression. 'It isn't a case of preference. I just thought you'd want to see her on your own.'

'With Anders around there isn't much chance of that anyway. He's what you might call the possessive type. Where Mother's concerned, he does have some cause to keep tabs, I admit. She's still a very attractive woman, and likes proving it.'

Tricia didn't care to probe that statement any further. Whichever way Leigh introduced her, it was going to be obvious to anyone with any insight at all that there was more to their relationship than that of simple employer-employee status. The only alternative was to insist on his dropping her off in Winterthur.

A problem she would face nearer the time, she decided. There was a whole night and morning to come first.

Leigh left her in no doubt of his intentions back at the hotel, following her into her room and closing the door behind him with a decisive and heart-jerking click. Double glass doors opened on to a balcony overlooking the lake. Tricia went out to view the scene, quivering when Leigh slid his arms about her from behind.

'Moonlight suits you,' he said softly. 'Your hair has silver streaks.'

'Probably premature grey,' she responded, and heard his low laugh.

'Only an Englishwoman would turn a compliment aside that way. You must know how lovely you are, Tricia.'

She said huskily, 'Isn't it said to be all in the eye of the beholder?'

'Only when blinded by love. You're beautiful in any light.' He pushed aside the hair at her nape with his lips to gently kiss the fluttering skin, hands seeking the curve of her breasts beneath her thin lacy blouse. 'Enough to drive any man to the brink!' he murmured.

Just a couple of glands, she reflected wryly, yet they appeared to constitute a major part of her attraction. Leigh was no different in that respect, it seemed.

'What is it?' he asked, as if sensing some change in her. 'Don't you like me touching you this way?'

'We might be seen,' she said, trying for a light note.

'Only by someone out there in a boat with night-glasses trained on this very spot,' came the dry reply, but he removed his hands anyway, moving forward to rest his arms along the rail at her side and direct an oblique glance. 'You'd feel better if you were flat-chested?'

He was too perceptive by half, she thought ruefully, and not one to be fobbed off with an evasive answer either. 'Not better, just perhaps a little more confident that it was me and not my "sweater-girl" profile that reckoned most.'

'I can't speak for others,' he said after a moment, 'but I can assure you that my own tastes cover a whole lot more ground. I thought I'd made that clear from the first. On the other hand, I'd be a liar if I tried to make out that your body doesn't do anything for me. It's the combination of intellect and looks that makes you so irresistible.'

On a temporary basis, at least, she reflected. Once they were back in England, it might well be a different story.

If she wanted to enjoy the rest of this trip she had to stop thinking ahead and take each day as it came, she told herself at that point. The nights too. Starting here and now.

Summoning a smile, she turned to slide her arms about Leigh's neck and press her lips lightly to one lean cheek. 'I'm being ridiculous!' she declared. 'Just forget I ever said it.'

He made no verbal answer, just pulled her closer and kissed her long and deep. Tricia gave herself over to the embrace, making no demur when he picked her up bodily the way he had done the previous time, and carried her indoors. Loving him the way she did, there was nothing she wanted more at this moment than to be with him again in every last sense of the word.

At the back of her mind was the slight fear that what she had said might make him a little reticent in his caresses, but she needn't have worried. His hands and lips were just as sure, just as wonderfully mindful of her pleasure as well as his own. He took her to the heights, satiated almost every last desire, and left her physically drained.

The only thing missing was his love, she thought bleakly when the connecting door closed in his wake some time later. And that he was under no obligation to provide.

Morning sunlight brought a whole new perspective. On a day like this, Tricia told herself, standing on the balcony to view the sparkling water already dotted with sails, it was impossible to feel anything but optimistic. The whole weekend lay ahead—theirs to do with as they liked. The only cloud on the immediate horizon, and that a relatively minor one, was Leigh's forthcoming visit

with his mother. She still had to sort out the question
of where she was going to spend the afternoon herself.

The two of them were among the first to eat breakfast
in the sunny restaurant. By eight-thirty they were out
amid the winding alleyways, old guildhouses and picturesque squares which scarcely seemed to have moved
forward since the Middle Ages.

The view from the Lindenhof was well worth the climb,
looking out over the spires and clustered roofs of the
old town to the river and lake and forested hills beyond.

'The fountain there commemorates a trick played on
the Habsburgs in 1292,' said Leigh. 'The men were out-
numbered, so the women donned uniform and manned
the battlements up here to give the impression of rein-
forcements. They saved the city. Inventive for that day
and age, wouldn't you say?'

'Inventive for any day and age,' Tricia laughed. 'But
then, we're a resourceful sex!'

'I'll go along with that.' He was smiling himself, eyes
holding an expression that brought a faint flush to her
cheeks as she met his gaze. 'Like old times again, isn't
it? Remember the sightseeing we did together back then?'

Tricia kept her tone light. 'How could I forget?'

'I imagine you've done a lot more travelling since?'

'I've been to Canada and Thailand,' she
acknowledged.

'Alone?'

'Yes.'

'A bit dangerous for a woman. Some situations out-
govern the equality theme, like it or not.'

'I never ran into any myself.'

'Sheer luck.' The pause was lengthy. When he spoke
again it was on a different note. 'Were you serious when
you said you'd consider working over here?'

'Isn't it about time we stopped thinking of it as us and them?' Tricia quipped, unwilling to commit herself to any kind of decision at this stage. 'We're connected to the mainland now.'

'But still possessed of an island mentality. It will take a long time for people to stop thinking of it as "going on the Continent", Channel tunnel or no. And you didn't answer the question.'

She kept her eyes on the scene below. 'Only because I didn't come to any hard-and-fast decision as yet. Paul's offer was an interesting one, I'll admit, but there's a lot to think about first.'

'Such as? You don't have any ties back home, do you?'

Tricia tried to make the shrug suitably casual. 'None to speak of. Footloose and fancy-free, that's me!'

'Supposing,' he said levelly, 'you were offered a permanent post in England. Would you consider it?'

'I already have been,' she returned. 'James Bryant is looking for a replacement when his secretary leaves. Always providing he was serious, that is.'

'Oh, he would be.' Leigh's tone was dry. 'You have all the qualifications. I was thinking more in terms of with Brinkland.'

It was only with difficulty that she kept her voice from reflecting her inner turbulence. 'Hardly suitable in the circumstances.'

'It could be.' He drew her round to face him, holding her with a light grasp on the upper arms. 'I don't want to lose you again, Tricia.'

The emotion that swept through her was overwhelming in its strength. He hadn't used the word love, but the intimation was there. Time was what mattered. Offering her a job was simply a means of ensuring she stayed around long enough for their relationship to evolve.

'It's worth thinking about,' she said softly, and saw the grey eyes take on a deeper hue.

'So think about it. Seriously.'

Tricia had the feeling that there was more he wanted to say, but there were too many people around now for any private conversation. It could wait; she could wait. There was always tonight.

They spent the rest of the morning exploring the maze of sleepy alleys and fine old buildings, such as the seventeenth-century town hall with its baroque Banqueting Hall, the Gothic Water Church boasting a superb Giacometti stained-glass window. Tricia was particularly fascinated by the confectionery shops on the Bahnhofstrasse whose wares were displayed like works of art themselves, so imaginatively decorative that it seemed a crime to disturb them.

'A month here wouldn't be long enough to see everything,' she declared over a luncheon of fish fresh from the lake at the little back-street restaurant Leigh had discovered on a previous trip. 'The nightlife alone must be among the best in the world.'

'It goes a fair way,' Leigh agreed. He both sounded and looked relaxed. 'Worth a longer visit, quite definitely.'

'Did you ever yourself?' Tricia asked. 'Spend more than a few days here, I mean.'

He shook his head. 'Never had the time. Monday, by the way, we'll be going out to Baden to take a look at this new company we acquired. It's going to be a pretty full schedule, I'm afraid.'

'It's what we're here for,' she said, and saw a glint spring in his eyes.

'Primarily.'

Looking at the lean, hard-boned face, Tricia felt swamped by love for him. She longed to say it, but it was neither the time nor place. Perhaps tonight she would find the right moment to tell him how she felt. Or then again perhaps she wouldn't. No rushing things. Let matters take their own natural course.

They picked up a hire car for the drive out to Winterthur. Set amid forested, castle-adorned countryside, the town was a commercial as well as a cultural centre. It was smaller than Tricia had anticipated, and bustling with weekend visitors.

Leigh turned aside her request to be dropped off, and drove straight through to a suburban woodland area scattered with fine villas, eventually turning in through opened gates to pull up before one of the finest.

Built like an oversized Swiss chalet and overlooking a small lake, the house took Tricia's fancy immediately. Money might not buy happiness but it certainly made life easier, she reflected, getting out of the car to stand for a moment looking out over the superbly maintained grounds.

'Not bad, is it?' said Leigh, coming round the car to join her. 'The Reison family settled here almost a hundred years ago. Anders is third generation Swiss.'

About to respond, Tricia's attention was drawn to the woman emerging from the house. Tall and slim, and wearing a plain though far from simple blue linen dress and pearls, she looked too young at first glance to be Leigh's mother. Hair the colour of freshly polished copper framed her strikingly attractive features.

'Darling, so glad you could make it!' she exclaimed. Blue eyes lost a little of their animation as they went beyond her son, who had moved forward to greet her,

to where Tricia stood. 'Oh, I thought you were bringing
your secretary?'

'I did,' said Leigh easily. 'Tricia's standing in for
Barbara.'

'Only on a temporary basis until she's fit to resume
work,' put in Tricia quickly. 'She had an emergency appendix operation.'

'Poor Barbara!' The sympathy sounded genuine. 'And
poor you, too, taking over at such a time. These business
trips are always so exhausting!'

'And how would you know?' asked her son on a note
of mild derision. 'You never went on one.'

'Imagination, darling,' came the light reply. 'Come
on through to the terrace, both of you. It's far too nice
a day to sit around indoors. Anders had to go to London
on Thursday, and won't be back until this evening, I'm
afraid. Still, it's perhaps as well, considering the way
you two tend to react towards each other. I really can't
understand why you don't like him, Leigh.'

'Can't you?' he asked drily. He slid a casual hand
under Tricia's elbow as she moved uncertainly forward
to follow the older woman, directing a reassuring smile.
'Dad sends his regards, by the way.'

Turning her head to answer, Helen Reison took in the
gesture with a faint narrowing of her eyes. The glance
she rested on Tricia's face was suddenly cooler. 'Do give
him mine.'

The house was as tastefully luxurious inside as out,
with rooms going off in all directions. Out on the broad
expanse of paved terrace at the rear there was a choice
of seats. Tricia took the shaded swing sofa only because
it happened to be nearest, but was glad all the same when
Leigh chose to join her.

They were seated so close that their knees were rubbing—he was obviously making no effort at concealment. Almost, Tricia thought, as if he was underlining the way things were between them. From the way his mother was looking at them, the message had certainly gone home. Approval, however, was not the message Tricia herself was receiving.

Conversation was far from easy, with Leigh making most contribution. Introduced as secretary, treated as personal companion, Tricia felt thoroughly out of place. Exactly what Leigh was playing at, she had no idea. All she did know was a growing anger with him for having placed her in such an invidious position.

Afternoon tea was served by a uniformed maid at four-thirty on the dot. One of the more civilised English habits she had never considered relinquishing, Helen acknowledged.

'I was talking with Jane on the phone only last week,' she remarked casually as she handed Leigh his cup. 'She told me what a wonderful time the two of you had at the Grainger girl's engagement party.'

'I can't say I found it such a riveting evening,' he replied so lightly that Tricia wondered if she had imagined the sudden tension in the thigh muscle brushing hers. 'Most of the people there were little more than kids.'

'Well, they'd obviously be young, wouldn't they, considering that Diane is only just twenty-two herself?' His mother sounded tolerantly amused. 'Really, darling, one would think you were in your dotage!'

'Just past finding much entertainment in that kind of affair,' he returned. 'You've put milk in this.'

'Oh, how forgetful of me!' She took the cup back from him, tipped the contents into the bowl provided for the purpose and poured afresh. 'There you are.'

The tea looked cloudy rather than black, but he made no comment. Tricia had the feeling that changing the subject had been his main object. Who exactly was this Jane? she wondered. More to the point, what was her place in his life? From the way his mother had spoken of her, they were on fairly intimate terms themselves, which seemed to point to a long-standing association. Yet how did that fit in with what he had intimated earlier regarding their own future?

Helen made no further reference to the matter, but turned the conversation in Tricia's direction, asking about her family and her life in general. Tricia responded politely, though with reserve, resenting the manner of what could only be termed an inquisition and angrier still with Leigh for not calling a halt to it.

It was only when he left them alone for a few minutes that his mother finally brought things to a head.

'I think I should warn you that my son isn't a free man,' she declared as soon as he was out of earshot. 'He's going to marry my god-daughter, Jane Davenport.'

There would come a time, Tricia knew, when this sudden and dreadful numbness would pass, but for now she had to take advantage of it. Her voice sounded remarkably cool and collected even to her own ears. 'Why would you consider I'd need warning, Mrs Reison?'

The older woman's smile was derisive. 'Do you think me incapable of recognising what you two have been up to? It's written all over you, my dear! I can't say I blame Leigh too much for taking advantage of the situation. You're a very attractive young woman. Just so long as you realise that there's nothing in it for you.'

Tricia's lifted eyebrow was a deliberate parody. 'I'm not looking for a husband, Mrs Reison. And, even if I were, I doubt if your son would be my ideal choice.'

'Really?' Helen Reison both looked and sounded sceptical. 'But you wouldn't deny you're having an affair with him?'

'Perhaps you should ask Leigh yourself. I'm sure he'd be delighted to have you take such an interest.'

'You already answered the question.' The older woman paused, expression revealing a grudging admiration. 'I must say, you're a very self-contained young woman. Far more so than I was at your age.'

All of it surface, Tricia could have told her. The numbness was giving way to a pain that threatened to become overwhelming. She fought to control it; sought refuge in anger. Leigh had played her for a fool again, just like the last time. How amused he must have been at the comparative ease with which he had coerced her into bed with him once more. It was all a game to him— a series of moves, like chess, at which he was no doubt also adept. There was a distinct possibility that he had recognised her almost at once and been drawn by the idea of relieving business pressures with a little self-indulgence.

With her point made, Helen reverted to the polite hostess and offered to refill Tricia's cup. The latter accepted because it gave her something to do with her hands. She felt no particular animosity towards the older woman, who had simply been making sure that she was under no illusions. Her hatred was directed solely at Leigh. He was going to pay for this. How, she wasn't yet sure, but no way was he ever going to know what foolish ideas she had entertained!

She was sufficiently in control of herself to offer him a brief smile in answer to the one he gave her on his return, and to keep up her end of the conversation over the following half an hour or so. They left at five-thirty, despite Helen's invitation to stay on for dinner.

'Anders will be looking forward to having you to himself after being away,' said Leigh with undisguised irony. 'I'd hate to deprive him. I'll see you next time I'm over.'

'Oh, before that,' returned his mother. 'I'm coming over myself next month to spend a week with the Davenports. Didn't Jane tell you?'

'Obviously not.' His tone was just a little short. 'Next month, then.'

Tricia kept her expression strictly neutral as she shook the hand extended to her. 'Goodbye, Mrs Reison,' she said coolly. 'Thank you for your hospitality. It's much appreciated.'

'You're most welcome,' declared the other, equally coolly. 'You'll no doubt have left Brinklands by the time I come to London.'

'I'll be going as soon as Barbara is fit to resume duties,' Tricia agreed. 'That should be around two weeks from now.'

'You have another job already lined up?'

'The agency will have. Or I might even decide to move overseas.'

'An excellent idea.' Helen gave her an approving nod. 'You could go far.'

And the further from her son, the better, Tricia gathered. She thought Leigh looked at her a little oddly as she slid into the passenger-seat, but he made no comment other than to remind her to fasten her seatbelt. Helen waved them off down the drive—a slim and elegant figure hopefully unaware that she had torn Tricia's whole world apart.

'Duty done,' Leigh said lightly when they were out on the open road. 'Now we can relax and enjoy the weekend our own way.' He slanted a swift glance when she failed to answer. 'Something bothering you?'

Tricia shook herself out of the depressive pit to summon a shrug and a moderated reply. 'I'm just a bit tired, that's all. It's been a long week.'

'With another to come,' he agreed. 'That's why we're going to make the most of this weekend together. I thought we might dine at the hotel tonight, and spend tomorrow taking in the sights. There's a wealth of old castles out here. Kyburg is one of the best, although Wuflingen is older. Dates back to the ninth century.'

'You'd make a good tour guide,' Tricia commented, and was aware that the sarcasm had not been muted enough when he gave her another swift glance.

'Good tour guides are born, not made. You really are tired, aren't you? Why don't you put your head back and take a nap until we reach the hotel?'

She shook her head. 'I'll feel worse if I do. A shower and a change of clothes is all I need to freshen me up again.'

'Plus an early night to catch up on some sleep?' The suggestion was accompanied by a smile that spoke volumes. 'Good for us both.'

Not the way he was thinking, vowed Tricia fiercely to herself. There would be no more lovemaking! Not with a man who was engaged to marry someone else. What an idiot she had been to put her faith in him not once, but twice! So far as Leigh Smith and his ilk were concerned, women in her position were fit only for affairs. When it came to choosing a life partner, they stuck to their own social levels.

Exactly how she got out of this situation without giving herself away was a problem she couldn't begin to deal with as yet. It was vital to her that she find some way of salvaging her pride. A bald refusal to share any further intimacies was unlikely to be accepted without good reason, and she had hardly given the impression of fading interest last night.

What she needed was time to set the stage for a strategic withdrawal, and time was what she didn't have. Leigh would expect to spend tonight the same way they had spent last night. Between now and then, she had to come up with some plausible excuse.

The hotel he had chosen was right on the edge of town. A converted country mansion, Tricia judged on viewing the Renaissance frontage and air of quiet elegance. The lobby was thickly carpeted and beautifully furnished, with several fine paintings on the pale cream walls. Clocks too, both simple and ornate—all showing the same time, she noted in passing.

It had occurred to her in the car that Leigh might have reserved just the one room in the circumstances. She was relieved to find that this wasn't so. There wasn't even a communicating door this time, although the rooms were adjoining.

'It's only a little after six,' he said. 'Why don't you take an hour to rest up before changing? I'll see you down in the bar around eight. OK?'

'Fine.'

Tricia could hardly wait to close the door on him, standing with her back to it to gaze numbly at the four-poster bed with its gauzy white drapery. She would have been in her seventh heaven had she not discovered what she had this afternoon. Right now she felt sullied by the very thought of Leigh's caresses.

The window looked out over gently rolling countryside to the distant mountains. She sank into a chair near by and sat viewing the scene while she tried to reach some decision on her actions from here on in. First and foremost was the need to conceal her true feelings from Leigh. With a further week of this trip still to come, and intimacy already established between them, that was going to be far from easy. The best way to manage it would be to claim the onset of her period. That might also serve to explain away her touchiness earlier. Deservedly frustrating too for a man anticipating another week of shared nights.

He actually anticipated more than that, she realised, recalling his suggestion earlier that she take a permanent job with Brinklands. 'I don't want to lose you again,' he had said, and she believed him. Where sex was concerned, they were, and always had been, perfectly attuned. But that was all he wanted from her; it was all he had ever wanted from her. Love didn't enter into it.

It was well gone seven before she finally stirred herself to get up and make some effort towards preparing for the evening ahead. She knew now how she was going to play the part, and actually looked forward to seeing the look on Leigh's face. His male ego was going to take quite a knock!

Wearing an amber silk jumpsuit belted in at the waist with gold kid leather, and matching high-heeled sandals, she made her way downstairs at ten minutes past eight to find Leigh already waiting in the lounge bar.

'I was beginning to think I should have given you a call,' he said. His smile approved what he saw. 'You look wonderful.'

'Spoken like a true gentleman!' Tricia quipped, surprising herself with the easy superficiality. She sat down in one of the silk embroidered chairs and took a swallow of the gin and tonic already awaiting her before launching on the prepared speech. 'By the way, I'm afraid I'm *hors de combat* for the next few days.'

Leigh's expression was difficult to define. 'The early warning is appreciated,' he said. He indicated the leather folder on the table. 'Have a look at the menu and see what you fancy. It's quite extensive.'

Somewhat nonplussed by his calm acceptance, Tricia followed the suggestion, reading down the list of dishes without actually taking in a word. 'I'll have whatever you're having,' she declared at length.

'Fine.' He summoned the hovering waiter with a crook of a finger, read off the required items in impeccable German and sat back on the man's departure to give her a thoughtful scrutiny. 'You're all on edge. Might it have anything to do what Mother said this afternoon?'

Too perceptive by half, she reiterated hollowly to herself. This was going to be even more difficult than she had thought. From somewhere she found the ability to flick an ironic eyebrow of her own.

'Women often are on edge, as you put it, at this time of the month. What exactly was it your mother said that's supposed to have upset me?'

'I'm not sure,' he returned levelly. 'But there was a definite atmosphere when I came back to the two of you.' He paused, still studying her with the same unnerving shrewdness. 'What did she tell you about Jane?'

Tricia's shrug was a masterful effort in the circumstances. 'No more than she thought I should know, considering our apparently obvious situation. She's a very astute lady!'

'Very,' he agreed. 'But that doesn't necessarily make her an oracle. Jane and I——'

'It really isn't important,' Tricia interjected. 'Not from my point of view, at least. Whether Jane would feel the same if she knew about this past day or two might be a different matter, but unless your mother felt moved to tell her I don't imagine she's ever going to find out.'

Leigh was looking at her as though he had never really seen her properly before, the line drawn deep between his brows. 'You really see our relationship as something quite separate from the one I have with Jane?'

Hearing him acknowledge it that way was a goad to the bitter rancour that filled Tricia. He wasn't even ashamed of the deceit he was practising on the girl he was to marry.

'What other way would I see it?' she heard herself asking without a single give-away tremor in her voice. 'There was never any question of our...affair being anything more than temporary. We're two people who happen to find each other physically attractive, that's all. It happens all over the world. I've no desire to be tied into a relationship, Leigh.'

He said slowly, 'You intimated that taking a permanent job with Brinklands was worth thinking about.'

'Which it is. Or was,' she amended.

'Then Jane does make a difference?'

'Only inasmuch as I'm not in the habit of carrying on affairs with married men.'

'You're not in the habit of carrying on affairs with men, period,' came the forceful reply. 'Don't give me that line, Tricia. It doesn't suit you!'

'You don't really know me,' she responded coolly. 'I'm not the naïve little Miss Nobody I was when we first met.'

'I never saw you as a Miss Nobody at any time.' There was nothing relaxed about his posture now; he both looked and sounded thoroughly antagonistic. 'But you're obviously right about not knowing you. I've been under the delusion that you were as genuine as they come!'

Tricia was too far into the role she had given herself to play to be capable of feeling any reticence now. 'Which just goes to show how false impressions can be. We make a fine pair, wouldn't you say?'

'All the way.' The grey eyes were cold as steel. 'Tell me, if you weren't *hors de combat*, as you so delicately put it, would you have been ready to carry on the way we were?'

With her throat hurting, it took everything Tricia had to retain command of her voice. 'Why not?'

It was a moment or two before he responded. When he did speak it was without expression. 'Why not indeed? In which case, we can look forward to utilising what time we have left before Barbara comes back to work.'

She had left herself wide open to that, Tricia acknowledged painfully as he picked up his glass with an air of dismissing the subject for the present. Short of giving herself away by leaving him flat here and now, she was stuck with the image she herself had created.

CHAPTER EIGHT

FAMOUS for its hot sulphur springs, and dominated by its ruined castle, Baden was also typically and prettily Swiss, until one reached the industrial quarter north-west of the town. Necessary to the economy, Tricia supposed, but ruinous to the environment.

Trailing in Leigh and Ulrich's wake as they toured the engineering factory along with a retinue of other personnel, taking notes as she went, she tried to keep her mind from dwelling too much on personal problems. Only four more days to get through after this, then home. Hopefully, Barbara might be ready to return to work herself the week following. Better a swift clean break than a drawn-out process.

They had returned to Zurich the previous evening after spending the day visiting the castles Leigh had spoken of. For Tricia every minute had seemed like an hour, though Leigh himself had shown little outward sign of constraint. What had been missing was the actual physical contact; he had made no move to so much as touch her shoulder when drawing her attention to some detail, much less put his arm about her as he had done before.

Having him think her as devoid of the finer emotions as he was himself had to be preferable to his knowing the truth, yet she hated the image. Keeping it up for another four days was going to be the hardest thing she had ever done. Seeing him now from the back, so tall and vital, made her ache with longing. Had she really been the type she had made herself out to be, the ache would have gone no deeper than mere physical deprivation. Perhaps there was something to be said for cultivating that approach to life.

It was Ulrich who solved the problem of what they should do with the evening by issuing an invitation to dinner at his home. From the alacrity with which Leigh accepted, Tricia could only assume that he too had not viewed the prospect of dining tête-à-tête again with overmuch enthusiasm.

'It isn't necessary to include me,' she said in an aside to Ulrich at a point when Leigh was involved in conversation with someone else. 'It's very kind of you, of course, and much appreciated, but I don't mind being left to my own devices.'

Ulrich eyed her shrewdly. 'You think you might be made to feel out of place in my home?'

'Oh, no, not at all!' She was anxious to deny any such intimation. 'I'm quite sure both you and your wife would go out of your way to make me as welcome as any other of your guests.'

'Then it's Leigh you don't wish to be with?'

Tricia attempted a laugh. 'Why on earth would you think that?'

'Something in the atmosphere between the two of you that wasn't there on Friday,' came the steady reply. 'I would say that you had had some kind of disagreement over the weekend which had nothing at all to do with work.'

Tricia could feel the warmth flushing her cheeks. She said very softly, 'Is it that obvious?'

'That you have a rather closer relationship than the purely professional?' His smile lacked censorship. 'Perhaps I simply recognise the symptoms. My wife was once my secretary. We were married less than six months after she took the job.' He added without haste or undue emphasis, 'Anne would be delighted to meet you. She's English herself.'

Put that way it was impossible to refuse, conceded Tricia wryly. Aloud, she said, 'I'll look forward to it.'

Returning to the hotel later, she said tentatively, 'I tried to get out of coming tonight, but Ulrich wouldn't hear of it.'

'What other plans did you have?' asked Leigh without particular inflexion.

'Well . . . none,' she admitted.

'Then why the reluctance in the first place?'

'I thought you might prefer to go alone, that's all.'

The strong mouth took on a familiar slant. 'Leaving Anne with the task of finding a lone woman to make up numbers? Not easy at short notice. Ulrich realises there's something going on between us, so obviously he'd expect you to be there. It doesn't tie you into anything.'

'Something going on between us'—that just about summed it up, thought Tricia painfully. Only not any more.

She wore the same green dress she had worn to the Munsters', only this time she left her hair up in its smooth French pleat. The le Tissier homestead lay about a mile or so outside the town along the lakeside. Timber-framed, and rambling in design, it had a covered veranda running along the whole rear elevation overlooking the lake.

'We both fell in love with the place the moment we saw it,' confessed Anne le Tissier over coffee. 'Far too large at present, of course, but we plan on adding to our family, God willing.' The smile she shared with her husband made Tricia yearn. 'The twins are demons, but they're a constant delight.'

The five-year-old twin boys had been in bed long before Leigh and Tricia's arrival. Devoted as they obviously were to their offspring, the le Tissiers didn't believe in showing them off to guests. Expecting a gathering, Tricia had been somewhat surprised to find that they were the only dinner guests. Not that she could fault the welcome Anne had extended.

Feature by feature the latter was no raving beauty, but she had a style and presence that gave the impression of being so. Tricia liked her—could imagine making a friend of her in other circumstances. She was one of those rarities, a woman who made no attempt to compete with others present: the total antithesis of Gerda Munster.

That Leigh liked her too was apparent. Liked her as a person, Tricia judged, not just because she was an attractive female. His attitude towards herself was pleasant and attentive enough now, but that vital spark was missing. Typical male double standards, she reflected cynically. It was fine for him to indulge a purely sexual desire, but unbefitting for a woman to do the same.

Not that he was unwilling to continue the association according to what he had said on Saturday night, approve or disapprove. It would be some slight satisfaction to close *that* door in his face when the time came.

Inevitably, conversation between the two men turned to business affairs. Anne moved her chair closer to Tricia's after a moment or two.

'I told Ulrich definitely no office talk tonight,' she said on a note of resigned humour. 'For what good it did! It seems that you and I must entertain ourselves for a while. What will you be doing next after this job finishes?'

Tricia kept her tone light, aware that Leigh might well have an ear tuned in their direction. 'It depends on what the agency comes up with. I rather fancy working overseas for a while.'

'Oh?' Anne looked surprised. 'I was under the impression——' She broke off, shaking her head as if in annoyance with herself, and said instead, 'Any particular part of the world?'

'Not especially. I'd probably stick to Europe these days.'

'Politically speaking, it might be safer,' the other agreed. 'I spent six months working in Kuwait before I came to Zurich, and had a wonderful time, but that's all gone now. If you're really serious, you should have a word with Ulrich. I'm sure he could help.'

'I don't speak German,' Tricia disclaimed. 'Just French and Italian.'

'Well, yes, that could be a problem. All the same, it would do no harm to mention it.'

'I'd as soon not, if you don't mind. Although I'm grateful for the thought.' Tricia sought a change of subject. 'How long have you and Ulrich been married?'

Anne conceded with grace. 'Seven years. Of course, he wasn't in the position then that he is now.' Her smile was reminiscent. 'I'd have married him whatever position he held. One look was all it took.'

Tricia knew exactly what she meant. Given the opportunity, it wouldn't matter to her either. Whether the same could be said of Jane Davenport was a question unlikely to be answered.

Returning to the hotel later, Leigh said levelly, 'You and Anne seemed to hit it off pretty well.'

'It would be difficult not to get along with Anne,' Tricia confirmed. 'She's a very nice person.'

'Unlike Gerda Munster.'

'As different as chalk from cheese.' She shot a glance at the hard-edged profile outlined against the streetlights. 'Why bring her into it?'

His shrug was deliberated. 'Three-way comparisons. There was a time when I'd have said you and Gerda were as different as chalk from cheese.'

'We are.' She kept her voice low to disguise the huskiness. 'I don't offer the same inducements.'

'You're not as obvious about it, I'll grant you, but the enticement is there all right. You play a man like a fish, Tricia.'

The unfairness of it took her breath. It was all she could do to speak at all, much less keep her calm. 'It makes a change,' she forced out, 'from being the one hooked! What do you have to complain about, anyway? You got secretary and bed-mate for the same price.'

His own indrawn breath was indicative of a flaring anger. 'If it's overtime you're after, name your figure!'

The pain was like a dagger through the heart. She wanted to rake her nails down the lean face—to see the blood flow. Controlling that impulse took everything she had.

'I think we should just forget the whole thing,' she managed after a moment. 'It was a mistake on both sides. I'll stick with the job until we get back to England, but if Barbara isn't well enough to take over by then you'll have to find someone else to type up the reports. My shorthand is pretty clear.'

'Fine.' Leigh was obviously making the same effort towards self-restraint. 'Consider it forgotten.'

Saying it was one thing, doing another, Tricia acknowledged dully. She hadn't succeeded the first time.

*   *   *

Beautiful, tanned, and elegant, Milanese women were
possessed of a sense of style that could turn a simple
chambray shirt and denim skirt into a chic ensemble by
adding a tailored jacket and good leather accessories.

'Few can afford to buy from such as Armani, Versace
or Ferre,' confirmed Vincenzo Barsini when Tricia expressed admiration of the look, 'so they make the most
of what they do have.' Dark eyes lit by an admiration
of his own, he added, 'You have style yourself, along
with a beauty to equal that of any of my countrywomen!'

Nice to hear, even if she didn't believe a word of it,
she thought, trying her best to ignore Leigh's sardonic
smile. It was Vincenzo himself who had insisted on her
accompanying the two of them to lunch. No table was
complete, he had declared, without a woman to grace
it.

The phrase 'laid-back' must have been coined with
the Italian male in mind, Tricia reflected now. Vincenzo
was in his fifties and had five children, the eldest of
whom was close to her own age, but that no more
cramped his style than did the presence of his superior
in the Brinkland hierarchy. Since first setting eyes on her
yesterday he had paid her the same extravagant court.

Last evening was the first she had spent alone since
the trip started. Whether Leigh had dined in his room
or gone out, she had no idea. Nor, she had tried to per-
suade herself, did she care. It hadn't worked, of course.
She did care. Very much so. Hiding it from him was the
main thing. Flirting with Vincenzo was one way, and
unlikely to be taken any more seriously by him than
intended.

'You,' she said lightly in Italian, 'are a born flatterer!'

'This is true,' he answered in the same language. 'But
only when the woman is worthy of the compliment. You

should come and work for me. Here you would be truly appreciated!'

'She's already considering Amsterdam,' put in Leigh drily, demonstrating his own command of the language.

'No contest,' came the prompt reply. 'Milan is the place to be. A beautiful and brilliant English secretary would make me the envy of all!'

'You already have a secretary,' said Tricia, treating the offer in the same manner in which she was sure it was extended.

Vincenzo lifted expressive shoulders. 'A detail I had overlooked, I admit. Perhaps you would like to become my mistress instead?'

Faced with those dancing eyes, it was impossible not to smile and answer in similar vein. 'I'll consider it very carefully.'

Leigh pushed back his chair to get to his feet. 'I've a phone call to make,' he said shortly. 'Excuse me, will you?'

His expression speculative, Vincenzo watched him cross the restaurant floor before turning his attention back to Tricia. 'I have the feeling,' he said, 'that our banter is not appreciated.'

'No sense of humour,' she returned, wondering who Leigh was calling. Making arrangements to meet someone tonight, in all probability. He would have female contacts everywhere. Men of his kind always did.

Vincenzo was looking at her now with that same speculation. 'I also have the feeling,' he said, 'that the association between you is somewhat more personal than it might appear.'

Tricia found a smile. 'Your instincts are way out this time. Personally speaking, we have very little in common.'

'You are a beautiful woman, and he is very much a man,' he declared. 'What else is needed?'

'A great deal,' she said. 'Women require more in a man than mere looks!'

'Tell me the qualities you consider necessary yourself?' he requested.

'Integrity, for one,' she said.

'And you find Leigh lacking in this?'

Tricia bit her lip, wishing she had turned the question aside with some flippant reply. 'I find most men lacking in it,' she came back weakly. 'I'd like to do some shopping if I get the chance before the stores close tonight. Can you recommend somewhere a little less pricy than the Via Monte?'

Vincenzo's shrug was good-humoured. 'You could try Fiorucci in the Galleria Passarella or La Rinascente in the Piazza Duomo, both of which, my wife assures me, offer good value. The shops are open until seven-thirty or thereabouts. Perhaps you would give me the pleasure of your company at dinner afterwards?'

Tricia looked him straight in the eye. 'Just the two of us?'

Totally unperturbed, he said, 'You do not care for the idea?'

'I don't believe in dining tête-à-tête with a married man,' she returned without caring how puritanical it might sound. 'In any case, I already made other plans.'

'A pity.' He sounded philosophical about it. 'I would much have enjoyed talking further with you.'

And the rest! she thought cynically. Vincenzo was no different from Leigh in that respect—just more open about it. Wives, fiancées, they were of minor importance when it came to indulging the baser instincts.

Leigh was coming back. Wearing the pale grey suit which sat his frame so well, he drew more than one pair of admiring female eyes in his passage. Tricia wondered if Jane was aware of his true character, or saw him as her knight in shining armour. If the latter, it was to be hoped that she never suffered disillusionment.

'We're taking the five o'clock flight to Paris,' he announced without preamble on regaining his seat. 'I'd like you to go back to the hotel to collect our bags, and meet me at the airport, Tricia. I ordered a taxi for you.'

It was the last thing she had expected, but it wasn't her place to query the decision. It was left to Vincenzo to do that.

'Why such sudden change of plans?'

The grey eyes gave nothing away. 'Something cropped up. I need to be back in London first thing Friday morning.'

Tricia was already on her feet. She put out her hand to Vincenzo. 'Goodbye, Signor Barsini,' she said formally.

He turned the hand and put it to his lips in a gesture unconstrained by the other man's presence. 'Goodbye, beautiful Tricia.'

She made her escape without so much as a glance in Leigh's direction. The taxi-cab was already waiting. Seated in the rear, she gazed out at the passing scene and wondered when, if ever, she would see the sights of Milan. Had she known they were to leave so soon she would have taken the opportunity last evening.

It could only be the call Leigh had made that had precipitated the decision to return home early, which suggested that it might well have been to Jane herself. It was even possible that his mother had dropped some hint to the girl regarding his extra-curricular activities.

Whatever the reason, they would be in England less than forty-eight hours from now, and, regardless of his apparent agreement the other night, she doubted if Leigh would be prepared to let her simply walk out on the job if Barbara wasn't yet fit to return. Even without his threatened blacklisting, it was hardly going to enhance her reputation with Profiles either.

She didn't really have much choice when it came right down to it, she concluded wryly. She had to see it through to the bitter end.

Reaching the hotel, she secured both room keys from Reception and asked for the account to be ready for signing in twenty minutes. Leigh's bag was packed but for the suit and shirt he had obviously planned to wear that evening, and his toilet items in the bathroom.

He still favoured a wet shave above the more convenient electric, Tricia noted as she repacked the compartmented bag. There had been one morning on the *Capucine* when she had lain and watched him shave through the opened bathroom door, loving the cosy intimacy of it. That would be Jane's prerogative in time to come—perhaps already was.

There was nothing to be gained from feeling bitter about it all, she told herself hardily, snapping the locks on the leather case. Leigh wasn't even worth the trouble of hating.

Declining to go to the trouble of ringing down for a porter, she carried both cases down to the lobby herself. The presented account included charges for two nights despite the fact that it was still barely three-thirty in the afternoon. Tricia briefly contemplated pointing this out, then shrugged and signed anyway. Company expenses were no concern of hers.

Another taxi was procured for the fifty-kilometre journey out to the intercontinental airport. Traffic was heavier now, with horns blaring out every few yards. What should have taken around forty-five minutes took closer to eighty. By the time they drew up outside the terminal building it was almost ten minutes to five.

Leigh emerged through the doors to pick up the bags as Tricia paid off the driver.

'We've had it for the five o'clock,' he declared with surprisingly little concern. 'I managed to get economy seats on a flight leaving at five minutes past six. That gives us time for a coffee—or would you prefer something stronger?'

Tricia shook her head. 'Coffee will be fine, thanks. Sorry about the delay. We crawled almost all the way here.'

'You can hardly control the traffic,' he said. 'It's of no consequence anyway.'

She slanted a swift glance as they stepped into line behind the couple already checking in at the desk. 'Then why the rush?'

'Policy,' he acknowledged without a flicker. 'I didn't like the ways things were shaping between you and Vincenzo.'

Voice taut, she said, 'That's ridiculous, and you know it!'

His shrug was brief. 'Let's just say I was taking no chances. If Vincenzo chooses to cheat on his wife that's his affair, but he's not doing it with a company employee. At least, not with my knowledge.'

The noise and bustle about them was sufficient to keep their conversation private; not that Tricia was in any mood to care at the moment. 'Different if he were a director, of course,' she said icily.

He looked at her then, an assessing glance that made her squirm inwardly. 'I'm not married.'

'Not far off. Neither,' she added, 'do I imagine it will alter your habits a great deal when you are!'

The grey eyes sharpened expression. 'I thought it made no difference to you either way?'

'It doesn't,' Tricia disclaimed hurriedly. 'I never had any illusions to be ruined.'

'But you think Jane might have?' The pause held deliberation. 'So why don't you give her the benefit of your experience? Go tell her what a rake she's mixed up with. It could get me out of a tight spot.'

Tricia stared at him, totally taken aback. 'What's that supposed to mean?'

The couple ahead moved off. Leigh lifted both suitcases on to the scale, and passed across the ticket file he had been carrying to the check-in clerk behind the desk—a job Tricia would normally have been doing. She stood there like a spare part while seats were allocated, directed a polite nod and a smile when the girl wished them a pleasant journey, and moved off at Leigh's side with the questions revolving in her head.

'Coffee first, then we talk,' he said.

Seated at a table for two some minutes later, he took a drink from his cup before launching into explanations.

'Jane is your age,' he said. 'I've known her all her life. Up until around six months ago I'd always regarded her as something like a younger sister, then she asked me to take her to a party out in Surrey somewhere as she'd fallen out with her boyfriend and didn't fancy going with anyone else.' He paused, mouth twisting. 'It was the first time I'd realised what a stunning young woman she'd become. Without going into detail, we finished up spending the night together—and quite a number more after that. Unfortunately, Jane's feelings for me developed into something more than I was prepared for. She took it for granted that marriage was the next logical step, and let her mother in on the act. I'm now under pressure from all sides.'

Tricia said slowly, 'There's no such thing as a forced marriage. Not in this day and age. If you genuinely don't want to marry her all you have to do is tell her so.'

'Considering the long-standing relationship between our respective families, and a very genuine regard, I'm finding that less than easy,' Leigh confessed. 'I've been living in the hope that she'd find someone else. I don't want to hurt her.'

'If she's in love with you, you can scarcely avoid it.' Tricia kept her tone level. 'Just don't expect me to do your dirty work for you.'

'A passing thought.' The grey eyes were veiled again. 'It would be better all round if she were to do the packing in herself rather than it come from me, that's all. Better for her, certainly.'

'Unless she's been living in cloud-cuckoo land all her life, she must have heard *something* of your reputation,' responded Tricia with irony.

'Reputations,' he said, 'are generally built on pure speculation. I'm no monk, but neither am I an out-and-out libertine.'

'You've obviously never been in love, though.' Her voice had acquired a slight huskiness.

'Not true.' He said it with a flat intonation more convincing than any emphasis. 'I've been let down twice. I'm not all that sure Jane's feelings aren't governed more by what she thinks she wants than what she really wants. We don't even have a great deal in common. She's a very immature twenty-five.'

Tricia's mind was still on that previous statement. For two women to have turned Leigh's love aside seemed almost impossible. What on earth could they have been looking for in a man that he had failed to provide?

'I'm sorry,' she heard herself saying without meaning to, and added hastily, 'For Jane, that is. I'm sure she deserves better.'

'I'm sure you're right,' came the dry agreement. 'And you? Do you deserve better?'

Her heart thudded painfully against her ribs. 'I wouldn't know.'

'Then think about it.' He looked up as the PA system crackled into life. 'That's our flight call.'

Think about what? Tricia wondered as she got to her feet along with him. Even if he succeeded in breaking things off with Jane Davenport, it would make little difference to her own position.

The plane was packed. Edging her way into her window seat, Tricia thought wryly of the extra space and comfort to be found in the first-class section, and was grateful for the reasonably short duration of the flight.

For a man accustomed to luxury travel, Leigh seemed singularly undisturbed by the lack of it, greeting the elderly French lady who took the aisle seat with an easy smile. He also, Tricia noted, supplied a few words of comfort when the latter revealed nervousness on take-off.

There was so much about him that was admirable, she reflected. He could be so thoughtful at times. She scarcely knew what to think about this thing with Jane. How could any man as pragmatic as he was in business allow himself to become entangled in such a manner? There was small comfort to be found in the fact that he wasn't, after all, in love with the girl. With two rejections behind him, it was doubtful if he'd let his emotions become involved ever again.

His suggestion that she help him escape the commitment by publicising their own involvement was a non-starter so far as she was concerned. If Jane loved him enough, she might find it in herself to forgive him even that. The intimation that, once free, he would want to continue seeing her, Tricia, she took with a pinch of salt anyway. What he'd had from her he could get from any woman.

He made no attempt to return to the subject during the flight. After clearing Customs at Orly they took a taxi to the hotel he had already advised of their early arrival.

'Supposing we put everything else aside for tonight, and just enjoy Paris?' Leigh suggested in the lift. 'That's if you feel up to it?'

It took her a moment to glean his meaning. Good liars had to have good memories, she reflected ruefully. 'I'm fine,' she said. 'But I——'

'No buts.' His tone was firm, his expression unrevealing. 'No commitment either. Just two people relaxing together.'

Relaxing was the last thing she would be doing, thought Tricia hollowly, unable to find a convincing reason to turn the offer down. She still had a part to play.

She wore the eternal little black dress, in this instance a sleeveless, figure-skimming silk jersey topped with the black-braided cream jacket from her two-piece.

'Very Parisian!' commented Leigh when he saw her.

Freshly shaven, and issuing a subtle, purely masculine scent, he devastated her senses to an extent she found difficult to conceal. She wanted badly to touch him, to feel his arms about her again, his lips on hers. She could empathise with Jane at this moment. It wasn't easy to come to terms with unrequited love.

Except that Jane wasn't aware yet that hers was unrequited. She was still living in cloud-cuckoo land. Tricia knew that feeling too. Twice over.

CHAPTER NINE

SILHOUETTED against a magnificent sunset, the Eiffel Tower had a grace and beauty Tricia had always found missing during daylight hours. She loved Paris as a city, although she felt little warmth towards its general populace, who tended, she felt, to treat all non-Parisians with scant courtesy. No matter how fluent one was in the language, the attitude remained the same.

'I've often felt I'd like to live here, but for the people,' she commented lightly, looking back at the sparkling watersprays of Palais de Chaillot. 'It has to be one of the most beautiful cities in the world!'

'Perhaps you're a little over-sensitive,' Leigh suggested. 'I never had any difficulty in getting along myself. You'll find Pierre Lamont the perfect gentleman.'

'There are exceptions to every rule,' Tricia agreed, not prepared to dispute the point. 'Shouldn't we be moving on? Our taxi driver will be able to retire on tonight's profits.'

Leigh gave her an amused glance. 'Tonight is on me personally, so you can stop worrying about the expense account.'

It was hardly her business anyway, Tricia conceded. She would soon be looking for another job. The thought brought depression; she shook herself out of it determinedly. For tonight at least, she was going to put all problems aside and make the most of every minute.

Dinner at Maxims had been an ambition since her very first visit to Paris. To have Leigh realise it for her went

147

beyond all expectations. Alighting from the taxi outside the world-famous restaurant, she had a lump the size of a golf ball in her throat.

Moving inside was like stepping back in time—an art nouveau world of mauve, green and mustard, of dim mirrors and exotic flowers. Leigh was greeted by name, and the two of them conducted like royalty to their comfortable banquette.

'I'm overwhelmed,' Tricia confessed, spotting several famous faces amongst the clientele. 'I could never afford to come here myself.'

'Lone women are frowned on anyway,' Leigh returned. 'An antiquated attitude maybe, but one that persists. How long do you plan on staying single yourself?'

The question took her by surprise. She found herself floundering for an answer.

'Until I meet Mr Right, I suppose,' she said on as flippant a note as she could manage. 'If I ever do.'

'And what qualities will *he* have to have?'

The same question Vincenzo Barsini had put to her, Tricia recalled, though in rather different vein. 'I don't have any rule of thumb,' she denied.

'Just someone you take one look at and fall madly in love with, is that it?'

The irony hurt all the more for its closeness to the truth. It had happened just like that three years ago, ruining her for anything less.

'Something of the kind,' she acknowledged on the same facile note. 'The whole shebang! Worth waiting for, wouldn't you say?'

'Always providing he feels the same way about you. Otherwise it could be a pretty devastating experience.'

The arrival of a waiter with their drinks cut through any reply she might have made. The cynicism had been there in the line of his mouth as well as the tone of his voice—the look and sound of a man thoroughly disillusioned. It explained a whole lot.

'How about you?' she asked. 'Assuming you don't marry Jane, that is?' She kept her tone nonchalant. 'After all, as the only son, you do have a duty to keep the name going.'

The strong mouth took on a further slant. 'I'd say there were enough Smiths left in the world without my contribution.'

'But hardly with the same blood running in their veins.'

'How do you know?' he countered. 'We might all have sprung from the same source way back.' He added smoothly, 'If you're so concerned for my family future, why not take the job on yourself?'

Tricia went cold inside. 'As a joke,' she said shortly, 'that's in a class of its own!'

Both expression and tone underwent an abrupt alteration. 'You're right. Forget it. This is supposed to be a friction-free evening. Did you look at the menu yet?'

She had hardly had the chance, Tricia could have replied, but that would simply be extending the friction. She turned her attention to it now, gazing at the words without taking them in. Had he been serious in the offer, she might even have considered it, she thought yearningly. How wonderful it would be to hold Leigh's child in her arms!

The service was superb. There must, Tricia reflected, be three waiters to every square metre! There was dancing too, although the floor space was only small. Replete on Sole Albert and heady with wine, she knew a growing urge to cast caution to the winds and take whatever *was* on offer. Leigh might not love her, but he still wanted her. What else did she have?

'Tomorrow night I'll introduce you to Tour d'Argent,' he said, almost as if catching her thought. 'Their *canard à la presse* is renowned.'

Tricia strove to keep her voice equally casual. 'The French may have other plans.'

'Too bad. Mine are already made.' He put down the glass he had been holding. 'Would you like to dance?'

'Love it,' she said, and knew she was saying yes to far more than that.

It was sheer bliss to be held close again after the deprivation of the last couple of days; sheer ecstasy to feel the warm strength of his embrace. Three years ago they had danced together every evening on board the *Capucine*—and later made mad passionate love. Tonight might well turn out the same. She wanted it to do so.

Recollection brought her up short. It was hardly going to happen while Leigh was still labouring under the impression that she was indisposed. Lies had a way of rebounding on the teller, she thought ruefully. Too late now to retract tonight.

She said tentatively, 'You told Vincenzo you had to be back in England first thing Friday morning.'

'A lie,' he admitted. 'As you must have realised by now. The original arrangement still stands. We'll spend the full day tomorrow with the French contingent, and leave Friday free. Do you know the Marais quarter?'

Tricia shook her head. 'Only by name. Hard to find, and even harder to find one's way around, I believe?'

'It can be. But well worth the effort. Pure seventeenth century. The place des Vosges dates back to 1612.'

She was cautious still. 'How do I get there?'

'With me,' he said. 'Unless you had other plans?'

Tricia nerved herself to look directly into the grey eyes. 'None better.'

A muscle tensed faintly along his jawline as he appraised her upturned face. 'That's more like the girl I once knew. What happened to her?'

'She grew up,' she said softly. 'Three years is a long time, Leigh. You've changed too.'

His smile was fleeting. 'Not to any extent. I wanted you then, I want you now.' He paused, added levelly, 'It might be just a physical attraction at present, but who's to say it couldn't develop from there? I think we should give it a chance.'

Tricia gazed at him with darkened eyes, fighting the temptation to say yes straight off. 'What about Jane?' she got out.

'I'm obviously going to have to tell her the truth.'

'She's going to be badly hurt.'

'Short of marrying her regardless, there's unfortunately no way of not hurting her. Anyway, it's my problem.' He waited a moment, mouth twisting. 'So, how about it? Do we take it from here, or call it a day?'

She said carefully, 'We could give it a try, I suppose.'

'Right.' There was no particular inflexion in his voice. 'I'll hold you to that.' He came to a halt along with the music, added steadily, 'Time we were making tracks, I think. Tomorrow's likely to be a heavy day.'

It was almost midnight when they left the restaurant. Leigh instructed their taxi driver to make a detour along the Champs-Elysées instead of making directly for the hotel. Paris by night was a fairyland, with the Arc de Triomphe rising in illuminated splendour above the tree-lined avenue. People still strolled the streets in the balmy air, or sat in relaxed conversation at pavement cafés. For many, the night was still young.

Secure in the darkened rear of the taxi, Tricia put up no resistance when Leigh slid an arm about her to turn her towards him. The kiss started soft and light, hardly more than a brushing of lip against lip, yet it fired an overwhelming response. The street-lighting was reflected in his eyes when he finally lifted his head.

'Just like old times.'

Not quite, she thought. The girl she'd been then had been blinded by the stars in her eyes. There was no guarantee now that Leigh would come to feel the way she wanted him to feel about her, but at least she wasn't under any illusions this time.

Saying goodnight outside her room door was doubly difficult when she knew it to be unnecessary. There was a moment when she was tempted to tell him the truth, but the words failed to materialise. Tomorrow she could plausibly claim to be derestricted again. She could wait until then. Just.

Pierre Lamont turned out to be everything Leigh had said of him. Small of stature, with the look of a certain French vocalist, he spoke English with the same captivating accent.

Tricia's French drew approbation from him. She was, he declared, that rarity with an ear for the subtler nuances of the language. They got along like a house on fire—as Leigh himself drily observed.

It was obvious to Tricia that the two men held each other in high esteem from both business and personal angles. It became obvious also, as the day wore on, that Pierre's secretary felt the same way about her boss as she did herself about Leigh. An occupational hazard when it came to men of their ilk, she supposed. That mixture of power and vibrant masculinity was irresistible.

'Has Simone been with the company long?' she asked casually on the way back to the hotel.

'About six years,' Leigh confirmed. 'The last two with Pierre.'

'I take it,' she said, 'that it's company policy to turn a blind eye to office affairs?'

'Providing it doesn't interfere with the job itself. The two of them are circumspect enough about it.' He cast her a swift glance. 'How did you guess?'

Tricia smiled and shrugged. 'Feminine intuition, I suppose. Is Pierre married?'

'Divorced. Twice, as a matter of fact. I doubt there'll be a third try.'

It took a real effort to keep her tone light. 'So Simone is unlikely to ever be more than an office affair?'

'She's married herself,' he said. 'Being a woman doesn't exclude her from fancying some extra titillation.'

'I think it could go rather deeper than that with her.'

'I wouldn't know.'

His tone was dismissive. Tricia took the hint and left the subject alone. Whatever the Frenchwoman's involvement with Pierre, it was no concern of hers either. She had her own problems.

There was a telegram waiting for Leigh at Reception. He opened the envelope in the lift, his expression undergoing a subtle alteration as he digested the contents.

'I'm afraid we'll be leaving early after all,' he advised on a suddenly brusque note. 'Try for a flight tonight if possible, will you?'

Tricia nodded, trying to conceal her churning disappointment. Further explanation was not, it appeared, going to be forthcoming, which, along with the fact that the telegram had come through here and not to the company offices, seemed to indicate a personal summons. One thing she wasn't going to do was ask. If it was anything to do with Jane Davenport, she didn't want to know.

She managed to secure two seats on the last British Airways flight at nine-thirty. Due to the time difference, they would be landing at nine-thirty too, which meant she should be home in Kingston by eleven at the latest.

Home. It seemed an age since she had last been there. She still had to sort things out properly with Neil. No matter what happened, that relationship had to finish once and for all. It should have done so long before this.

They had dinner in the airport restaurant rather than risk a last-minute dash. Leigh was quiet—almost introspective, Tricia thought. She made little attempt to fill the pauses in conversation herself.

'I imagine you're wondering what this is all about?' he said at last over coffee. He reached into an inside pocket to take out the envelope he had received earlier, face expressionless. 'You'd better read it for yourself.'

The message was short, its impact numbing: 'Pregnancy confirmed. Must see you soonest. Love, Jane.'

Green eyes lifted to meet grey, expression carefully controlled. 'It seems an odd way of letting you know. Did you have any idea this might be on the cards?'

'No,' he denied. 'Not that it makes any difference.'

Tricia kept a tight hold on her emotions. 'Meaning you're going to feel honour-bound to marry her after all?'

He gave a wry shrug. 'What's the alternative? I'm no believer in abortion, and I can't leave her to bear the brunt alone.'

She said levelly, 'Do you think she might have done it on purpose?'

'Either that, or sheer carelessness. One of the dangers in delegating responsibility. Whichever, it happened.'

'It could be worse,' she said. 'At least you won't be marrying someone you have no feelings for at all. Who knows? It may turn out to be the best thing you ever did!'

'Sure.' He studied her for a moment, eyes veiled. 'What about you?'

Her shrug was as philosophical as she could make it. 'I'll survive.'

'Without a doubt. You'll still stay on until Barbara gets back?'

'I'll finish the job, of course,' she said, afraid of giving too much away by refusing, the way every instinct in her prompted her to do. 'Do you want me to stay in town again next week?'

'Better if you do,' he agreed. He looked down at the brandy glass in his hand, mouth slanting. '"The best laid schemes . . ."'

Tricia's throat felt as tight as a drum skin. 'I'm sure everything will work out all right,' she managed on an amazingly level note. 'I assume you rang Jane to tell her you were on your way?'

Leigh shook his head. 'I'll be with her soon enough.'

It was going to be well gone ten by the time they cleared Heathrow, but it was his decision to make, Tricia told herself. The thought of returning home to the flat with this hanging over her was depressing in the extreme. To-morrow she would at least have work to keep her mind occupied—and plenty of it.

Their flight was delayed more than half an hour, which didn't help matters. Leigh had little to say. Unlike many men caught in the same situation, he was making no attempt to evade liability—an attitude Tricia was forced to admire. Jane would probably never know how close she had come to losing him.

The time was just coming up to a quarter to eleven when they finally made it through Customs at Heathrow. It was raining hard, the air chilly after the continental warmth.

'You're not taking the train this time of night,' Leigh stated when Tricia attempted to take her leave. 'I'll drive you out to Kingston.'

'It isn't necessary,' she protested. 'I'll be fine. In any case, you have to go to Jane.'

'Too late now,' he declared. 'It would be gone midnight by the time I got there. Tomorrow will do.' He indicated the ramp leading to the car park. 'Let's go.'

Short of refusing point-blank, she had no choice but to go along with him. She didn't even know where he lived himself, she realised. As a bachelor, he probably had an apartment, but that would all change, of course, when he married Jane. With a wife, and child to come, he would need to start looking for a proper home.

Like deliberately teasing an aching tooth with her tongue—that was what she was doing, Tricia acknowledged wryly at that point. She had to put it all behind her and start afresh. Leigh wasn't the only man in the world!

He put the heater on in the car to drive out the damp chill of a fortnight's standing. Relaxing into the soft leather seating, with the swishing wiper-blades making more noise than the sound-proofed engine, Tricia closed her eyes and willed herself to doze off in order to get the journey over as quickly as possible. So far she had managed to keep her end up, but for how much longer she could maintain control over her emotions was anyone's guess. The last thing she needed was to have Leigh realise how she really felt about him at this stage.

He switched on the radio when they were clear of the airport, trying all stations until he found some music.

'That's better,' he said. He glanced her way. 'Tired?'

'A bit.' Tricia could hardly trust her voice. 'It's been a long day.'

'Too long,' he agreed. 'And tomorrow promises to be longer still.'

'I suppose,' she said, 'that the wedding will be very soon.'

'Before anything starts to show, you mean?'

She bit her lip. 'Sorry, that was badly put.'

'There's nothing to apologise for,' he said. 'If I know Mrs Davenport, she'll already have arrangements under way.'

'Without waiting to find out how you feel about it?'

'Like my mother, she leaves nothing to chance.' Outlined by the sodium lighting, the lean profile looked austere. 'I can't blame anyone but myself. If I'd kept my hands off in the first place, there wouldn't have been any problem.'

'It takes two,' Tricia said softly. 'Jane is old enough to know what she was doing.'

'Like you?' There was irony in his voice. 'Did you know what *you* were doing?'

Her brows drew together. 'About what?'

'Taking this job on without telling me who you were. Was it your idea from the start to make me pay for this man who let you down?'

She said thickly, 'Pay how?'

'By leading me to think we might have a future together.'

Tricia swallowed hard on the dryness in her throat. 'I wasn't the one doing the leading. You set it all going again. And what kind of a future were you proposing? Something like Simone and Pierre?'

It was several seconds before he answered. His tone was muted. 'I was looking towards eventual marriage. The surface recognition might have been missing initially, but it was there right enough underneath. I let you go three years ago because I thought you were only interested in a holiday affair. This time I wasn't going to give up so easily.'

She could hardly get the words out. 'Why tell me now?'

'Pure masochism,' he admitted. 'It probably wouldn't have worked out anyway. You're still in love with whoever it was who let you down, aren't you?'

Tricia felt as if an iron band had fastened across her chest. 'It was you,' she whispered. 'Don't you realise that? It was you!'

There was a lay-by coming up. Leigh turned into it without indicating, earning himself a prolonged horn hoot from the car behind.

'Say that again,' he commanded.

'What's the use?' Her voice sounded choked. 'It's too late.'

He turned her towards him with hands that felt like vices. 'I don't care. Just tell me!'

She gave way because she wanted to—because she needed to get it all out in the open. 'I thought *you* were the one who only wanted a holiday affair. You gave me no real reason to believe anything else. It took me a long time to get over you—or at least to convince myself that I had. I persuaded myself that I could handle it when I realised who you were, only it didn't work.'

'You put on a very good act,' he said gruffly. 'The physical attraction was obviously still there, but I couldn't seem to get any closer.' He looked at her with desperation in his eyes. 'There has to be some way round this!'

'There isn't,' she said. 'Not without leaving Jane in the lurch. You wouldn't do that, any more than I'd want you to.'

'There are times,' he growled, 'when doing the right thing takes second place to personal priorities. I can't let you go, Tricia. Not now!'

'You have to.' She was close to breaking down altogether. 'What's the alternative? Set me up as your bit on the side?' Her throat closed up again at the look on his face. 'Oh, God, I'm sorry! I didn't mean that the way it sounded. Only what else is there?'

He made a sound low in his throat and pulled her to him to kiss her with a passion that would have been frightening in its intensity if she hadn't felt the same way.

'We could at least have tonight,' he murmured against her lips. 'Just tonight!'

She wanted to say no, but the word wouldn't form itself. One night of real love. Was that so much to ask? Jane was going to have everything else.

'Just tonight,' she heard herself repeating.

Neither of them said very much during the rest of the journey. Tricia tried to keep herself from thinking about tomorrow, and all the other tomorrows to come. She'd got through before, she would get through again. There would eventually be someone else for her—someone who would come to mean as much to her as Leigh. There had to be!

The flat seemed smaller than ever. Tricia switched on a light without looking at Leigh, who stood with her suitcase still in his hand.

'Shall I make some coffee?' she asked huskily.

He dropped the case to the floor and came over to pull her into his arms, kissing her into a state where nothing else mattered but the fact that they were here together.

'There'll never be anyone else I feel this way about,' he said fiercely. 'I won't give you up, Tricia!'

She said nothing because there was nothing to say. He knew as well as she did that this was all they were going to have. Come the morning he would be gone, so they must make the most of the present.

It was Leigh who switched on the lamp in the bedroom. 'I want to see you,' he said. 'I want to remember every last detail.'

He undressed her slowly, caressingly, exploring each and every inch of her with a touch that made her quiver both inside and out. She did the same with him, running her hands over the broad shoulders to feel the muscle ripple, kissing her way through the tangle of hair on his chest, loving the taste of him, the male scent of him, the pure masculine power. All man, and, for the moment, all hers.

They spun out the foreplay until neither of them was able to wait a moment longer. Tricia clutched him with feverish fingers as he came over her, drawing in her breath at the exquisite sensation as they slid slowly and smoothly together. To be possessed this way by the man she loved was everything wonderful. She wanted to hold him there inside her forever.

Impossible, of course. Her body was already responding, hips lifting, moving in rhythm with his, all thought blanked out in the surging torrent of emotion as he carried her up and over the crest into a place where nothing at all existed.

There was a brief moment as the world steadied again when she thought she was back on board the *Capucine*. Realisation was a black cloud pressing down on her. This was all she would ever have of Leigh. Once he left here tonight he was lost to her. She didn't think she could bear it.

'We shouldn't be here like this,' she heard herself saying. 'It's only making things worse.'

The dark head stirred on her shoulder, lips seeking the pulse-point where shoulder merged into neck. 'There's only one way we can make things any better,' he said roughly, 'and you already vetoed it.'

'You mean carrying on a relationship on the quiet?'

'Yes.'

Tricia swallowed painfully. 'I can't do it, Leigh. I couldn't face sharing you with your wife. I want what she's going to have—a husband, a proper home, children of my own.'

He lifted his head to look at her, eyes dark. 'They're more important to you than I am?'

'That's not fair,' she protested. 'The way I feel about you isn't the issue. I'm just not capable of living with the kind of arrangement you're talking about. If you really feel the way you say you do about me, you won't expect it.'

'I'm desperate enough to try any recourse,' he confessed. 'I know now how an animal must feel in a trap. I don't love Jane. I never could love Jane. Not the way

I should. What kind of life is that going to be for either of us?'

'One you have to make the best of,' she said huskily. 'For your child's sake if nothing else. A lot of marriages start off in similar circumstances.'

'And most of them fail for the same reasons.' He kissed the corner of her mouth, moving up along her cheek to press his lips to each closed eye. 'I need you, Tricia. I realise I'm being thoroughly selfish, but I don't care. I'll do whatever it takes to keep you!'

The temptation to give in and go along with him was almost overwhelming. She wouldn't be the only one by a long chalk to settle for what she could get. With care, Jane need never know about it.

But *she*, Tricia, would know, came the dulling thought. She would be the one waiting for Leigh to come to her, never daring to make any arrangements of her own in case he turned up unexpectedly. How long, anyway, before he tired of such an arrangement himself? How long before love turned to resentment of the demands she made on his time? To lose him that way would be worse than a clean break now.

'I'm sorry,' she said. 'It just wouldn't work.'

For a moment he made no movement at all, then he rolled abruptly away from her to sit up and reach for his things. Tricia lay watching him numbly as he dressed.

'I'll see you some time tomorrow,' he said without looking at her as he drew on his jacket. 'You might check on Barbara's progress in the morning. She should be out of hospital by now. You'll find her number on file.'

Tricia made no reply. The coming week promised to be the most difficult time of her life, but it had to be got through.

He left without speaking again. Considering her flat refusal to comply with what he had asked of her, she didn't suppose there was anything left to say. She was on her own again in every sense.

CHAPTER TEN

GETTING to work via British Rail proved the usual trial. It was almost nine-thirty when Tricia finally reached the office.

Leigh would be on his way to Jane by this time, she judged. She wondered if he could possibly feel as dispirited as she did herself. He at least had someone who cared for him. That had to be better than nothing.

She had to stop this self-pity, she told herself harshly. It was doing no one any good. She might never meet anyone else who could make her feel quite the way Leigh made her feel, but that wasn't to say she had to spend the rest of her life alone. There were different kinds of love—different kinds of men. At twenty-five, she had time enough to find her Mr Right.

Because she was involved in transcribing her notes, it was gone eleven before she realised that she still hadn't telephoned Barbara. Her home number, as Leigh had said, was on file. Dialling it, Tricia hoped for a favourable response to the question of when the woman would be fit to return to her job. The sooner the better, so far as she herself was concerned. The longer she had to stay on here, the harder it was going to be, both for her and for Leigh.

The voice which answered the call sounded crisp and efficient and reassuringly healthy.

'I'm calling on Mr Smith's behalf to ask how you are,' said Tricia. 'He had to be out this morning, or I'm sure he would have called himself,' she added, sensing some element of disappointment in the silence. 'I'm the temp standing in for you, by the way.'

'I rather gathered that,' returned the other. 'You can tell Mr Smith that I'll be coming in to see him next week. Perhaps you'd take a look at his appointments and tell me when he's likely to be free?'

'Of course.' A little puzzled, Tricia reached for the desk diary and swiftly scanned the entries for the week. 'Wednesday morning is clear at present.'

'Then put me down for ten-thirty, will you, please? It's essential that I see him personally.' There was a pause, and a change of tone. 'I assume you accompanied Mr Smith on the Euro trip in my stead?'

'Yes, I did,' Tricia confirmed.

'How did it go?'

'Very well. Few problems. I just got started on the report.'

'Really?' The note had altered again. 'I usually have mine more or less completed by the time we return.'

'I don't work overtime.' It was all Tricia could think of by way of excuse on the spur of the moment. 'At least,' she amended, 'not unless it's absolutely essential.'

Barbara's laugh sounded brittle. 'I admire your fortitude. You must have had plenty of time left to sightsee.'

'Well, yes.' Tricia was cautious. 'Paris was the only city out of the five that I'd visited before. It was quite an opportunity. You must know them all pretty well yourself, I imagine?'

'Probably not as well as you do.' The crispness was back. 'Wednesday at ten-thirty, then.'

Frowning a little, Tricia replaced the receiver. It seemed strange that Barbara would need to make an appointment to see Leigh when all she had to do was say when she would be back.

Unless there had turned out to be complications of a kind she wouldn't want to discuss over the telephone. Appendicitis had been the original diagnosis, but that wasn't to say it had been the correct one.

Whatever happened, there was no way she herself was going to stay on after this week. Someone else must be found to take over if Barbara couldn't return. If Profiles couldn't come up with another job immediately she would have to try the other agencies.

The two appointments scheduled for this morning had been postponed to next week, leaving the two-thirty and three p.m. ones *in situ*. At two o'clock Tricia was on the verge of cancelling those too. Leigh's arrival saved her the trouble.

'Sorry,' he said. 'I meant to be here before this. Did you get any lunch yet?'

'I made myself a sandwich and coffee,' she confirmed. 'Your father called. Shall I get him for you?'

'Not just yet,' he said. 'I could use some coffee myself.'

'I'll bring it through.' She came to her feet, moving round the desk to make for the alcove, every nerve in her tensing when he put out a hand to grasp her shoulder. 'Leigh——'

He made no sound, just pulled her roughly into his arms and put his mouth to hers in a kiss that hurt. It was impossible to fight him. Impossible to do anything but kiss him back with the same desperate passion. She leaned against him weakly when he at last lifted his head, knowing she should move yet unable to summon the will.

'This is stupid,' she whispered. 'Utterly stupid!'

'It might be all of that,' came the roughened return, 'but it's the way things are. I can't stop wanting you just for the telling.'

'Just wanting?' It was all she could do to get the words out.

He held her a little away from him to look into her eyes, his own darkened and intense. 'I love you,' he said. 'I never told *any* other woman that. If I hadn't made such an almighty mess of things, we'd be looking to a future together ourselves.'

'Don't.' She felt torn in half by the desire to hear him say it and the despair engendered by the words. 'I'd rather not think about it. How did it go with...Jane?'

He took his cue, letting her go and stepping back from her with features tautly drawn. 'As you'd expect. The wedding will be next month. Register office. I drew the line at the kind of ceremony her mother had in mind. The quieter, the better, so far as I'm concerned.'

'Yes.' It was all she could find to say. 'I'll get the coffee.'

He was standing at the window when she went through. Wearing a dark blue suit she hadn't seen before, along with a crisp white shirt, he looked every inch the executive. Jane would surely be the proudest woman alive to have Leigh Smith for a husband, Tricia thought numbly. She knew she would have been.

'Your coffee,' she announced unnecessarily. 'I rang Barbara, by the way. She made an appointment to come in and see you on Wednesday morning.'

Leigh swung to look at her, a line drawn between the dark brows. 'An appointment? What on earth for?'

'To talk about returning to work, I imagine.'

'She'd hardly need to see me to tell me that.' The frown was still there. 'Did she seem all right?'

Tricia placed the cup and saucer carefully on the desk. 'So far as I could tell over the phone. Perhaps she simply needs more time and thought it only right to come and discuss it with you personally.'

It was evident from his expression that he thought that as unlikely as she did herself. 'You could phone her back,' Tricia suggested.

Leigh shook his head. 'It will wait till Wednesday. What's on the agenda?'

'Appointment with a Mr Peters at two-thirty, followed by a Mrs Hunt at three. And there's your father's call.'

'I'll make that later,' he said. 'Right now, he's the last person I want to speak to.'

'You think he might know already?' she asked.

'Mother will have seen to that. I, apparently, was only told after everyone else was put in the picture.'

Gathering support, thought Tricia bleakly. Jane couldn't know the father of her child all that well if she had imagined that she had to bring family pressure to bear. Leigh didn't shirk his responsibilities. He would try to make this marriage work out, she was sure, even though his heart wasn't in it.

She made her escape from the office before she gave way altogether. Cliché or not, life had to go on.

Mr Peters arrived on time, and was leaving as Mrs Hunt arrived. An attractive, well-dressed woman in her thirties, she gave the impression of being in total control over every facet of her life. Tricia envied her that assurance.

Taking in the tea requested in preference to coffee, she was struck by the air of familiarity between Leigh and his visitor. Another of his past affairs? she wondered dully. By his own admission, he had been no monk in the past. For Jane's and their child's sakes, it was to be hoped that he could find it in himself to stay faithful in the future.

There was no word from within after the woman had left. The phone call at four from James Bryant came as a complete surprise. Tricia had never really expected him to follow up his interest.

'I'm holding you to that dinner date,' he said. 'How about tonight?'

For a moment she was tempted to say yes. Anything to take her mind off things. But that would hardly be fair on James.

'Sorry,' she said. 'Not tonight.'

'Tomorrow, then. Or, failing that, any night you *can* manage, this week, next week, whenever!'

The laugh was forced from her. 'You really don't give up easily, do you?'

'Not when the challenge is worthwhile.' He paused. 'Is it just me you don't want to be with, or some prior commitment?'

'I have no commitments,' she said, and steeled herself against the pain of that statement. 'All right, next Friday.'

'Good.' He sounded well satisfied. 'Eight o'clock at Inigo Jones.'

'Inigo Jones,' she repeated, trying to sound enthusiastic. 'I'll be there.'

Leigh was standing in his office doorway when she looked up after replacing the receiver. His face was expressionless.

'Not wasting any time, I see.'

The coldness in his voice was a whiplash. 'So what am I expected to do?' she asked defensively. 'Sit around pining for someone I can't have?'

'It doesn't have to be like that. Not if you don't want it to be.'

She looked back at him with something approaching hatred for what he was doing to her. 'I told you last night, I can't live that way. If you can't understand why, I'm sorry!'

For a moment he remained there gazing at her with the same fixed expression, then the coldness dissolved into wry acknowledgement. 'I do understand. I just can't take it, that's all. That was James Bryant on the phone just now, wasn't it?'

Tricia saw no point in denying the fact. 'I half promised to have dinner with him after we got back from Europe.'

'To discuss the job offer?'

'He didn't mention that.'

'But you'll take it if he does?'

She shook her head. 'I think it might be best all round if I went away. Far away.'

'Like Amsterdam, for instance?'

Her laugh sounded cracked. 'Where I'd be likely to run into you every six months or so? Hardly a practical solution. Mrs Carrington mentioned a job that may be coming up in Bermuda next month. Some millionaire who thinks his memoirs worth recording. Not really my kind of thing, but worth considering. Who knows? I might even find myself a rich husband. As they say, off with the old love, on with the new!'

'Why not?' Leigh's face was taut again. 'Maybe that's all you wanted in the first place.'

The hurt of it was like a shaft through her heart. 'In which case,' she flung at him, 'you had a lucky escape, didn't you?'

The opening of the outer door cut short any reply he might have made. Framed on the threshold, Adam Smith looked from one to the other of them with faintly lifted brows as he sensed the atmosphere. Tricia came to her feet in automatic deference to his position, controlling the trembling in her limbs with an effort.

'Mr Smith, I——'

'I was about to return your call,' cut in his son shortly. 'You didn't have to come in.'

'Patience was never a family virtue,' came the un-moved rejoinder. 'I'm here now, so let's get on with it.'

Leigh stood back to allow his father entry to the inner office, affording Tricia the barest of glances before closing the door. She heard the sound if not the content of conversation through the thickness, which meant both voices had to be raised above normal tones. Leigh was putting right any wrong he had done, she thought in swift defence of the man she loved. What use was there in parental railing?

Whatever words had passed between father and son, the former showed no sign of agitation on emerging from the office again some ten minutes or so later. He paused by Tricia's desk to take a comprehensive look at the VDU, nodding approval of the page on show.

'Well formulated,' he said. 'You're obviously accus-tomed to doing the donkey work in presentation. I hope my son didn't keep you too busy while you were in Europe?'

Whether the innuendo was intentional or not, it cer-tainly came across as such. Tricia kept her eyes fixed firmly on the screen, her voice as steady as she was able to make it. 'No more than was necessary, Mr Smith. I had plenty of time to look around.'

'Good.' He continued to hover for a moment as if on the verge of saying something else, then he gave a faint shake of his head and moved on.

Tricia drew in a quivery breath as the door closed in his wake. He knew. How, she wasn't sure, but he knew! Not that it made any difference now anyway. The affair was well and truly over.

The inner office door remained firmly closed over the following hour. Apart from a couple of calls she put through, the two of them had no communication at all. If she stayed on for a couple of hours, Tricia reckoned, she could have the report finished, leaving the next week free for general purposes. Whether Barbara herself was returning or not, she was finished here altogether next Friday night. Dinner with James would be her first step towards a new start.

There was still no sign of departure on Leigh's part when the telephone rang again at five-fifteen. The voice on the other end of the line asking if Mr Smith was still there was young and female; it scarcely needed the addition of a name to disclose the identity of the caller.

'Putting you through now, Miss Davenport,' said Tricia tonelessly, depressing the switch.

The urge deep inside her to continue listening was so strong that she could hardly resist it. Only on the words, 'Leigh, darling, it's me,' did she find the will to replace the receiver in its rest before she could hear any more. Jane sounded...nice. She must be, or Leigh would surely never have been drawn to her in the first place. They would make a perfect couple, sharing the same kind of background, the same friends. Their interests might differ a little, from what Leigh had said in Winterthur, but they would no doubt learn to compromise.

She was deliberately twisting the knife again, Tricia acknowledged painfully. Whatever they made of their life together, it was no concern of hers.

The extinguishing of the extension light on the telephone was followed moments later by Leigh's emergence from the office. Eyes unrevealing, he said, 'I thought you'd gone.'

'I'm staying to finish this,' she answered without looking up. 'I'll have a print-out ready for you on Monday morning. Enjoy your evening.'

'You too,' he said. 'Give James my regards.'

He was gone before she could form a reply, leaving her sitting there aching. He obviously thought she was seeing James tonight. No wonder he had been cynical about her speed of recovery. Even given the opportunity, there would have been no point in putting him straight.

She had decided to stay at home rather than suffer the anonymity of a hotel room over the weekend, even if it meant suffering the vagaries of the rail system; she was accustomed to it anyway. It was gone nine when she eventually reached the flat, to find a message from Neil on the answering machine, cancelling their Tuesday date for next week without giving any specific reason. Tricia hoped he had found someone else. She had been a coward in not breaking off the relationship herself the moment he had showed signs of becoming serious.

The weekend provided little in the way of rest and recuperation. Facing the same packed out journey again on Monday morning, she felt jaded before she had even started. It had never really bothered her all that much in the past, she admitted, strap-hanging all the way into town. Just an unavoidable part of the working day. The

Bermuda job would at least free her from all this for a few months. It might even prove interesting.

Leigh kept his distance all day. He dictated letters with crisp efficiency, appended his signature without comment and generally treated her like a piece of office furniture. Hurtful, she was bound to acknowledge, although probably best for them both. Employer, employee, that was all they were to each other now. And that only until the end of the week.

Tuesday and Wednesday were no easier. Leigh was out of the office when Barbara Graham arrived at ten twenty-seven, leaving Tricia to make lame excuses for his absence.

'I'm in no particular hurry,' the older woman assured her, taking a seat and picking up a magazine from the rack. 'I can wait.'

Wearing a tailored dress in dark green, with a string of beautifully matched pearls as her only jewellery, she epitomised the popular image of the perfect secretary. Attractive in an understated kind of way, with her smoothly styled fair hair and regular features, Tricia thought, but different altogether from what she had anticipated.

'How do you like the job?' asked the other, glancing up from the magazine.

Tricia made every effort to dissemble. 'Fine. You must be eager to get back to it yourself.'

'I shan't be coming back.' It was said calmly enough, though with a trace of regret in her voice. 'I shouldn't really be telling you before I tell Mr Smith, but you'd know soon enough.'

'I'm sorry.' Tricia scarcely knew what else to say. 'Are things so bad?'

Barbara looked blank for a moment, then she smiled and shook her head. 'Nothing to do with the operation. At least, not directly. I'm getting married.'

Tricia exerted iron control over her facial muscles. 'Congratulations. Someone you met recently?'

'No.' Her smile this time had a wry cast. 'I had time and opportunity while I was in hospital to take a long hard look at my life. This job *was* my life. I put it before everything else. All very well right now, but it won't always be there. I've left it a bit late to think about starting a family, but hopefully not too late.' She closed up suddenly, obviously regretting the confidence. 'I imagine there's a very good chance that you'll be offered the job yourself. Shall you take it?'

Tricia shook her head. 'I have something else already lined up.'

Leigh's arrival cut short any reply the other might have been about to make. 'Good to see you, Barbara,' he said as the woman came to her feet. 'Sorry to keep you waiting. Come on through.' His glance shifted briefly to Tricia. 'Bring coffee in, will you, please?'

'Of course,' she said expressionlessly.

The two of them were seated in the comfortable chairs provided for informal gatherings when she went in with the tray. It was difficult to tell Leigh's reactions to the news from his face, although it must have come as something of a shock to him. Barbara herself seemed composed enough on the surface, but Tricia suspected an entirely different picture beneath. Was fear of a lonely old age a good enough reason to marry a man one didn't love? she wondered bleakly. Perhaps in years to come she might eventually think so.

Leigh buzzed for her to come through almost immediately after Barbara left. He was seated at his desk again, lean fingers toying with a pencil. Looking at him, Tricia yearned for the right to go to him, to put her arms about him, press her lips to his. Rather a lonely old age than settle for anything less.

'Barbara isn't coming back to work,' he said. 'Which leaves me in something of a dilemma. Would you consider staying on until a replacement is found?'

'No!' The refusal came out sharper than she had intended. She made an attempt to modify her tone. 'No longer than Friday. I'll naturally leave everything in order.'

'Hardly everything.' The irony was heavy. 'As you didn't ask why Barbara isn't coming back, I gather she already told you the reason?'

'She's getting married.'

'Right. Something of a surprise, I have to admit. She never mentioned any serious relationship.'

'Possibly because it wasn't up until now.' Tricia swallowed on the lump in her throat. 'If that's it, I'd better get on.'

'It isn't.' He came to his feet, framed against the glass wall at his back, features set in lines of determination. 'Tricia, we can't let it go like this. I *won't* let it go like this! We have to work something out.'

'There's no way we can. Not without leaving Jane to fend for herself.' She put up a hand as he made a move. 'No, Leigh, don't! It's no use!'

He paid no heed. Go, said the voice of reason as he came round the desk, but her feet stayed rooted to the spot. She wanted this as much as he did, regardless of the rightness or wrongness of it. Just to feel his lips on hers again, the warmth and comfort of his arms about her—a few stolen caresses; Jane could surely spare her that much.

Only it didn't stop at that, of course. It couldn't. Passion overtook resolution the moment he touched her. She clung to him as he pressed her down on to the sofa, kissing him feverishly, wantonly, eager for the burning touch of his hands on her bare flesh as he unfastened her blouse right down the front. His mouth followed, tongue a flickering flame that threatened to consume her. She held his head to her, pressing her lips into the thick dark hair, loving him, wanting him, needing him. Only when he put a hand to the zip of her skirt did she come to her senses.

'We shouldn't be doing this,' she whispered painfully. 'It isn't fair to any of us.'

'I don't care about being fair,' he said roughly. 'I can't go through with it, Tricia. Not feeling the way I do. I love you, not Jane. I have to tell her the truth!'

For a wild moment Tricia allowed hope to take over, but only for a moment. 'You can't,' she said. 'Not now. Who knows what she might do if you walked out on her? Would you want to take the risk of her having the baby aborted?'

'No,' he admitted. 'I'd just have to make sure she didn't.'

'How? By getting a court injunction? It's *her* body, Leigh.'

'And my child!' The fierceness went out of him suddenly; she felt it go. He pushed himself abruptly away from her, ran a hand through his hair in a gesture that said it all. 'You're right, of course. It would be her decision.' His eyes went over her as if storing up the memory. 'You're not going to change your mind either, are you?'

Tricia shook her head, biting down hard on the urge to give in to what he was asking. He might tell himself it was what he wanted, but he would have more than enough to occupy his time in family and job.

She felt sordid as she buttoned up her blouse again. A secretary and her boss having sex—or almost—on the office sofa! She was being unfair to them both, she knew, but something in her wouldn't let up. The whole situation was shameful.

'It's almost twelve,' she said unsteadily. 'I'll take early lunch, if that's all right?'

'Fine.' Leigh was in full command of himself again. 'I'm out to lunch myself at one, so I probably shan't see you until later this afternoon.' Just for a moment, as their eyes met, he seemed to waver, then his jaw firmed. 'We'll need to advertise the position. There's no one else here I'd care to work with on any permanent basis. Perhaps you'd talk to Personnel when you get back.'

'Will do,' she said.

Reaching the outer office, she stood for a moment with eyes closed and heart heavy while she steadied herself. She could see the image etched on her retina against her eyelids: Leigh's face in close-up, every detail sharp and clear. She would carry that memory with her for all time.

The personnel officer expressed surprise that she wouldn't consider taking on the job herself. Most people, she said, would be only too delighted to be offered such an opportunity.

'You've proved yourself more than capable of handling it,' she declared. 'Mr Smith isn't easy to please, but he seems well satisfied with your performance.'

Don't read innuendo where none was intended, Tricia told herself. No one else knew about her and Leigh. Only his father, and he was unlikely to have spread it around.

'I prefer change,' she responded equably. 'I'll probably be going overseas next.'

'Really?' The woman looked interested. 'Where to?'

'Bermuda.' The job wasn't yet secured, but Mrs Carrington had said it was hers if she wanted it. Whether she took it or not was still a question to be resolved, but there was no need for anyone else to know that. 'Working for a millionaire property tycoon.'

'Lucky you!' There was frank envy in the comment. 'How come he can't find a secretary in his own back yard?'

'I didn't ask,' Tricia admitted. 'All I know is that he contacted Profiles to find him someone willing to spend six months working out there.'

The other laughed. 'I'll bet there was no shortage of takers! I'd have considered it myself, given half a chance. Anyway, I'd better ask Mrs Carrington to organise a replacement for you as from Monday. It's going to take some time to find the right person to take the job over permanently—especially as Mr Smith will want to vet the short-list for himself.'

Tricia was glad to make her escape. The very thought of someone else working with Leigh was depressing. Friday couldn't come soon enough.

It was back to distance-keeping on his return at three. For all the reaction he showed, this morning might never have happened, thought Tricia disconsolately. Perhaps he had finally reconciled himself to his position. Better for him if he had. Better for Jane too. Better for everyone except herself. She was right out in the cold.

Thursday brought some relief in the sense that it was her next to last day. The fact that in a little over twenty-four hours she would be saying goodbye for the last time was something she didn't want to think about too deeply as yet.

Leigh was due in a meeting at eleven. He would be lunching with the chairman afterwards, he informed her formally. Tricia took her lunch break at twelve-thirty, avoiding the staff restaurant in favour of a café across the road. Rumour of her refusal to take on the job full time had spread like wildfire, no doubt giving rise to all kinds of speculation as to why she should turn down such an excellent position. She didn't feel up to facing it.

She took a table near the door, ran an uninterested eye over the menu, and settled on a tuna salad as the least likely dish to choke her. Someone took the chair opposite. Looking up, Tricia saw a girl around her own age gazing across at her with an odd expression in her eyes. The table next door was free, she noted. Why intrude on *her* privacy?

'You're Leigh's temporary secretary, aren't you?' said the newcomer. 'Tricia Barton?'

Tricia gazed back in frozen silence for a long moment, taking in the other's long blonde hair and pretty features. Not unlike the way she had looked herself three years ago, came the fleeting thought.

'Yes,' she said. 'That's me.'

There was a long indrawn breath, as if to steady over-stretched nerves. 'I'm Jane. Jane Davenport. You might have heard my name?'

Tricia gathered her wits. Her smile felt rigid. 'Of course. You and Leigh—I mean, Mr Smith—are going to be married.'

'He's told you that himself?'

Tricia hesitated, sensing a pitfall. 'Actually, it was his mother who told me,' she said. 'Over a week ago, in Winterthur.'

The breath was drawn again. 'She shouldn't have done that!'

'Why not?' Tricia put on a puzzled expression, feeling a total fraud. 'It's true, isn't it?'

'Yes. Only it——' Jane broke off, biting her lip. Opening her handbag, she took out a photograph, studying it herself for a second or two before sliding it face up across the table. 'That's you, too, isn't it?'

The snap showed a young blonde-haired girl standing at the rail of a ship, face tanned by the sun and lit with laughter. The *Capucine's* resident photographer had snapped her in passing, Tricia recalled, catching her at a moment when happiness had been spilling over. She'd forgotten all about it, until now. Where on earth had it come from?

'Does it look like me?' she prevaricated.

'Not initially, no, but the features are the same.' Jane's voice was ragged. 'That fell out of a wallet Leigh dropped last night. He doesn't know I've got it. Until I saw you just now, I'd no idea who the girl was. There's a date on the back. Three years ago.'

There was little use, Tricia decided hollowly, in continuing to deny the identity. 'All right, it is me,' she said. 'It's a long time ago. Nothing to worry about now.'

'If that's true, why was he carrying it around with him after all this time? And how is it that you're working for him now?'

'Coincidence. Just pure coincidence, that's all.' Tricia tried a laugh. 'He didn't even recognise me at first!'

'But he hasn't altered very much in three years. *You* must have recognised *him*.'

'Well, yes, I suppose I did.' She was getting in deeper and deeper, Tricia acknowledged. The only thing for it was the truth—or as near as she dared come to it. 'I didn't think it mattered. As I said, it was all a long time ago. I'd no idea he was carrying that around. In all probability, he'd forgotten he had it himself.' She forced a lighter note into her voice. 'Few men reach Leigh's age without having had a number of past girlfriends.'

'It isn't so much the past that concerns me,' came the uneven reply. 'I came here today especially to see you. I knew Leigh was lunching with his father, and I intended coming up to the office, but the hall receptionist said you were on your lunch break. She pointed you out to me when you came out of the lift, so I followed you across here.'

Tricia looked back at her with assumed non-comprehension. 'Why would you want to see me if you didn't even realise it was me in that photograph until just now?'

'Because my godmother warned me there might be something going on between you and Leigh, and I needed to know what you looked like.' She paused, searching Tricia's features with an intensity that seared. '*Is* there something going on?'

If she answered yes, Tricia thought, it wouldn't alter anything for the better. She held the gaze without flinching. 'No.'

'I don't believe you.' The statement was flat. 'I might have done if I'd never seen that photograph, but not now. Just tell me one thing. Do you love him?'

There was no stopping the flooding heat in Tricia's face, the involuntary contraction of muscle in her jawline. Jane needed no further confirmation; that was obvious from her expression. 'And Leigh,' she continued inexorably. 'Does he love you?'

Tricia made a valiant attempt to regain some command of the situation. 'No, he doesn't. You're the one he loves.'

'I'm the one he's going to marry,' Jane corrected in that same unemotional tone. 'And only then because he feels obligated.' She pushed back her chair and stood up, face set in lines of determination. 'There's something I can do about that.'

'Jane, no!' Tricia was on her feet too, mind racing ahead to draw the obvious and dismaying conclusion. 'You're wrong. You really are wrong! Please don't go doing anything you'll regret!'

The smile was wan. 'If you mean abortion, you don't need worry. I'm glad I came. I knew all along it wasn't going to be any good. You're in no way the kind of person Leigh's mother made you out to be.'

People around were ignoring the two of them with typical London incuriosity. Tricia sank down nervelessly into her chair again as Jane left. Regardless of what Leigh had said that morning, he wasn't going to back out on his responsibility. The marriage would go ahead, the baby would be born, and the two of them would work things out together. There was no other way.

It was gone three o'clock when Leigh finally put in an appearance. He looked different, Tricia thought—as if a weight had been lifted from his shoulders.

'There's something I have to tell you,' she said before he could speak. 'Jane came to see me at lunchtime.'

'I know. She told me.' He indicated the inner office door. 'Come on through. We've a lot to talk about.'

Heart hammering, Tricia got to her feet and preceded him into the other room. Jane had known Leigh was lunching with his father; she must also have known where. That was the only way she could have contacted him in the short time that had passed since their meeting in the café. Something I can do about that, she had said, but a refusal to marry him was hardly going to resolve the problems.

'I didn't tell her about us,' she defended as he closed the door at her back.

'I know that too,' he said. 'My mother did. I hoped she would at the time.'

She turned sharply to look at him, searching the grey eyes in growing confusion. 'I don't understand.'

'It's simple enough, if not very forthright. I wanted them all to realise that my interests lay elsewhere. I thought it might hurt Jane less to hear it that way than for me to tell her to her face—at least allow her to be the one to finish it.' His smile was wry. 'Pure cowardice, if I'm honest. However, what I hadn't taken into consideration was Mother's determination to see the marriage go through. It was she who talked Jane into sending that telegram.'

Tricia said slowly, 'Are you saying it wasn't true?'

'Yes. She dragged me away from the lunch table to confess. I'd realised she'd been on edge since I got back, but I put that down to her condition. What it really was was guilty conscience. It's probable that she wouldn't have gone through with it even if she hadn't met you.'

Tricia was still trying to take it all in. 'Unless she was prepared to fake a miscarriage or something, the truth would have come out eventually anyway.'

The strong mouth slanted again. 'Mother covered that aspect too. By that time the marriage would already be a fact. She knows my views on divorce. For me, it would have to be the very last resort. I saw what it did to Dad when she walked out on him. She had the nerve to phone him and suggest he make sure I gave you the push right away.'

'Do you hate her?' Tricia asked softly.

'No,' he said, 'I don't hate her. I've learned to accept that it's just the way she is. Anders isn't the man she left us for. She'd pack him in too if something more interesting came along, although age is starting to catch up on her now, I suppose, so they might go the distance.' His shrug dismissed the subject. 'I'm more concerned with our future right now.'

Tricia could still scarcely believe that they had one. She went into his arms like a homing-pigeon, meeting his lips with a fervency matched by his own. The whys and wherefores didn't matter at the moment, only the fact that it was all working out for them.

'How did you get that photograph?' she asked some time later. 'I thought I had the only copy myself.'

'I got the photographer to run me another print off,' Leigh admitted. 'I looked it out after I left you the other night. I'd kept it locked away as my only tangible souvenir of that cruise. If I'd looked at it recently I might have recognised you earlier than I did.'

Head pillowed on the broad shoulder, secure in the warm strength of his arms at last, Tricia was feeling no pain. 'There was a point where I almost walked out after I recognised you,' she said. 'Just think, we might never have got together again at all.'

'Chance,' he agreed. 'Or fate. We should have had the sense to see it three years ago.'

'We were both under a misapprehension. Anyway,' Tricia added softly, 'it's all in the past.' She hesitated. 'How will your father take it, do you think?'

He laughed. 'With great relief. He approves of you totally. He called me a damned fool for letting you get away from me in the first place.'

Tricia lifted her head to look into the grey eyes, her own widening. 'He knows about the *Capucine*?'

'Not every detail, but I told him how we met. He's very fond of Jane, of course, and blames me wholly—and quite rightly—for the whole fiasco, but he didn't see the marriage working out either. He'll be looking for a grandchild at the earliest opportunity, I warn you.'

'Then we'll have to try and oblige him,' she said. Her voice took on a tremor. 'I love you so much, Leigh!'

His eyes kindled afresh, arms tautening about her. 'And I you. More than I can find words to say right now. You're everything to me, Tricia.'

Her laugh came low. 'For a man without words, you don't do at all badly!' She put a hand to the lean brown cheek, heart overflowing as he turned his head to press his lips against her palm. 'What about work? Is it against company policy for your wife to act as secretary?'

'Is that what you want?' he asked.

'Until such time as it becomes necessary for me to give it up.' She paused. 'Always providing you wouldn't find it too much to be together all day?'

'All day and all night, I could never find it too much!' he declared with certainty. 'We've three whole years' separation to make up for just for starters.'

And a whole lifetime to do it in, she thought as he found her lips once more.

HARLEQUIN®

PRESENTS *plus*

Meet Helen Palmer. She knows that as *single* mother of the bride, she's going to have to spend time with Zack Neilson, *single* father of the groom. Trouble is, Zack's the man responsible for her broken heart.

And then there's Charlie MacEnnaly. When it rains it pours! Not only is she forced to accept the hospitality of business tycoon Phil Atmor—her only neighbor on Norman's Island—she's forced to bunk in with Sam, Phil's pet pig.

Helen and Charlie are just two of the passionate women you'll discover each month in Harlequin Presents Plus. And if you think they're passionate, wait until you meet Zack and Phil!

Watch for
MOTHER OF THE BRIDE by Carole Mortimer
Harlequin Presents Plus #1607

and

SUMMER STORMS by Emma Goldrick
Harlequin Presents Plus #1608

Harlequin Presents Plus
The best has just gotten better!

Available in December wherever
Harlequin Books are sold.

PPLUS7

Take 4 bestselling love stories FREE

Plus get a FREE surprise gift!

Special Limited-time offer

Mail to Harlequin Reader Service®

3010 Walden Avenue
P.O. Box 1867
Buffalo, N.Y. 14269-1867

YES! Please send me 4 free Harlequin Presents® novels and my free surprise gift. Then send me 6 brand-new novels every month, which I will receive months before they appear in bookstores. Bill me at the low price of $2.24 each plus 25¢ delivery and applicable sales tax, if any*. That's the complete price and—compared to the cover prices of $2.99 each—quite a bargain! I understand that accepting the books and gift places me under no obligation ever to buy any books. I can always return a shipment and cancel at any time. Even if I never buy another book from Harlequin, the 4 free books and the surprise gift are mine to keep forever.

106 BPA AJJA

Name	(PLEASE PRINT)	
Address	Apt. No.	
City	State	Zip

This offer is limited to one order per household and not valid to present Harlequin Presents® subscribers.
*Terms and prices are subject to change without notice. Sales tax applicable in N.Y.

UPRES-93R

©1990 Harlequin Enterprises Limited

POSTCARDS FROM EUROPE

HARLEQUIN PRESENTS®

There's a handsome Greek just waiting to meet you.

THE ALPHA MAN
by Kay Thorpe

Harlequin Presents #1619

Available in January wherever Harlequin books are sold.

HPPFEG

Hi!
Spending a year in Europe. You won't believe how great the men are! Will be visiting Greece, Italy, France and more.
Wish you were here—how about joining us in January?

HARLEQUIN  PRESENTS®

A Year
DOWN UNDER

In 1993, Harlequin Presents has celebrated the
land down under. In December, let us take you
to New Zealand—our final destination—in
SUCH DARK MAGIC by Robyn Donald,
Harlequin Presents #1611.

Simple friendship isn't possible between Philip Angove,
a wealthy New Zealand station owner, and
Antonia Ridd. First, he wants her to put her
professional ethics aside. And then there's the fact that,
although the man simply exudes sex appeal, Antonia's
met his kind before and she's therefore determined to
avoid his so-called charms. But Philip is equally
determined to make that hard for her to do!

Share the adventure—and the romance—of
A Year Down Under!

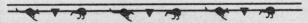

Available this month in
A Year Down Under

RELUCTANT CAPTIVE
by Helen Bianchin
Harlequin Presents #1601
Available wherever Harlequin Books are sold.

YDU-N

Harlequin is proud to present our
best authors and their best books.
Always the best for your
reading pleasure!

Throughout 1993, Harlequin will bring you
exciting books by some of the top names in
contemporary romance!

In November, look for

BARBARA
DELINSKY

First, Best and Only

Their passion burned even stronger....

CEO Marni Lange didn't have time for nonsense like
photographs. The promotion department, however,
insisted she was the perfect cover model for the launch
of their new career-woman magazine. She couldn't
argue with her own department. She should have.

The photographer was a man she'd prayed never
to see again. Brian Webster had been her first—
and best—lover. This time, could she play
with fire without being burned?

Don't miss FIRST, BEST AND ONLY by Barbara Delinsky...
wherever Harlequin books are sold.

BOB6

1993 Keepsake

CHRISTMAS

Stories

Capture the spirit and romance of Christmas with KEEPSAKE CHRISTMAS STORIES, a collection of three stories by favorite historical authors. The perfect Christmas gift!

Don't miss these heartwarming stories, available in November wherever Harlequin books are sold:

ONCE UPON A CHRISTMAS by Curtiss Ann Matlock
A FAIRYTALE SEASON by Marianne Willman
TIDINGS OF JOY by Victoria Pade

ADD A TOUCH OF ROMANCE TO YOUR HOLIDAY SEASON WITH KEEPSAKE CHRISTMAS STORIES!

HX93